THE TEXAS TATTLER
All the news that's barely fit to print!

Marine Sergeant Drafted for Operation Parenthood!

Every hot-blooded female in Red Rock has been talking about how to get her hands on that dishy new Fortune heir, Sergeant Sam Pearce. And it sure looked as if heaven was smiling down on the women in this little Texas town when Sam became a daddy to his friends' twin daughters. But now it looks as if Michelle Guillaire has beaten out the stampede of wife wannabe's and come to this overwhelmed bachelor's rescue!

Yup, ladies. In between planning Miranda Fortune's much-talked-about wedding to her long-ago love, Michelle also manages to effortlessly care for these motherless toddlers. And though Michelle is burning the candle at both ends, there's definitely a glow to her.

Is this Texas family about to prove yet again that where there's a Fortune, a true-bred Texas love is sure to follow?

Dear Reader,

Welcome to Silhouette Desire! We're delighted to offer you again this month six passionate, powerful and provocative romances sure to please you.

Start with December's fabulous MAN OF THE MONTH, *A Cowboy's Promise.* This latest title in Anne McAllister's popular CODE OF THE WEST miniseries features a rugged Native American determined to win back the woman he left three years before. Then discover *The Secret Life of Connor Monahan* in Elizabeth Bevarly's tale of a vice cop who mistakenly surmises that a prim and proper restaurateur is operating a call-girl ring.

The sizzling miniseries 20 AMBER COURT concludes with Anne Marie Winston's *Risqué Business,* in which a loyal employee tries to prevent a powerful CEO with revenge on his mind from taking over the company she thinks of as her family. Reader favorite Maureen Child delivers the next installment of another exciting miniseries, THE FORTUNES OF TEXAS: THE LOST HEIRS. In *Did You Say Twins?!* a marine sergeant inherits twin daughters and is forced to turn for help to the woman who refused his marriage proposal ten years before.

The sexy hero of *Michael's Temptation,* the last book in Eileen Wilks's TALL, DARK & ELIGIBLE miniseries, goes to Central America to rescue a lovely lady who's been captured by guerrillas. And sparks fly when a smooth charmer and a sassy tomboy are brought together by their shared inheritance of an Australian horse farm in Brownyn Jameson's *Addicted to Nick.*

Take time out from the holiday rush and treat yourself to all six of these not-to-be-missed romances.

Enjoy,

Joan Marlow Golan

Joan Marlow Golan
Senior Editor, Silhouette Desire

Please address questions and book requests to:
Silhouette Reader Service
U.S.: 3010 Walden Ave., P.O. Box 1325, Buffalo, NY 14269
Canadian: P.O. Box 609, Fort Erie, Ont. L2A 5X3

Did You Say Twins?!

MAUREEN CHILD

Published by Silhouette Books
America's Publisher of Contemporary Romance

Special thanks and acknowledgment are given
to Maureen Child for her contribution to
THE FORTUNES OF TEXAS: THE LOST HEIRS series.

 SILHOUETTE BOOKS

ISBN 0-373-76408-1

DID YOU SAY TWINS?!

Visit Silhouette at www.eHarlequin.com

Printed in U.S.A.

MAUREEN CHILD

was born and raised in Southern California and is the only person she knows who longs for an occasional change of season. She is delighted to be writing for Silhouette Books and is especially excited to be a part of the Desire line.

An avid reader, Maureen looks forward to those rare rainy California days when she can curl up and sink into a good book. Or two. When she isn't busy writing, she and her husband of twenty-five years like to travel, leaving their two grown children in charge of the neurotic golden retriever who is the *real* head of the household. Maureen is also an award-winning historical writer under the names of Kathleen Kane and Ann Carberry.

THE FORTUNES OF TEXAS

Meet the Fortunes of Texas

Meet the Fortunes of Texas—a family whose legacy is greater than mere riches. As the family gathers to thank four special people who stood by Ryan Fortune in his hour of need...three special gifts ignite passionate new romances that only a true-bred Texas love can bring!

CAST OF CHARACTERS

Sam "Storm" Pearce: This gunnery sergeant thought the battle began when he took on twins. But when he sends for reinforcements, he's in for the fight of his life...to keep the woman he never stopped loving!

Michelle Guillaire: This wedding planner is used to celebrating other couples' joyous occasions, but will she let a dark secret now stand in the way of her second chance at love?

The Crier and The Spitter: These twin sisters' lives have been upended enough by their parents' deaths, so don't they deserve a family?

One

"**O**kay," Gunnery Sergeant Sam Pearce told himself as his gaze raked across what looked like miles of shopping aisles. "Let the battle begin."

An older woman, coming into the store right behind him, rammed her shopping cart into his backside and when he turned to stare at her, gave *him* a dirty look.

"Excuse me, ma'am," he said, instinctively apologizing.

"For heaven's sake," she said, nodding her head so sharply her pink hat tilted onto her forehead. "Doesn't the army teach you any better than to stand in a doorway?"

"I'm a Marine, ma'am," he corrected her and tried not to wince at her unintentional insult. Civilians, he reminded himself, pretty much couldn't tell a Marine from a Sailor from a military-school cadet.

She reached up and pushed her hat back into place, then narrowed pale-blue eyes at him. "Son," she snapped, "I don't care if you're Captain Kirk off the Starship Enterprise. I've got bingo to get to and you're in my way."

Hell, he knew better than to slow down a woman on a mission. "Yes ma'am," he said, and stepped aside.

Deliberately, she huffed out a breath, and steered her cart around him. As she went past, he heard her mutter, "Darn fool. Shouldn't allow men into grocery stores. They only get in the way."

He was with her on that one, Sam thought and moved further out of the path of the next oncoming cart. A young mother with a screaming two-year-old in the basket gave him a harried smile as she swept past him.

He *was* in the way. Nothing he hated more than shopping, which is why he usually got his groceries from the corner convenience store. A man could live on hot dogs and frozen burritos. But his life was about to change, he reminded himself as he snatched a cart free, and it wasn't as if he had a choice now, was it?

His hands fisted on the cold steel bar tight enough

to grind it into dust. Grumbling under his breath, Sam told himself to treat this shopping trip as he would a military mission. Scope out the terrain, find what he needed and get out. Hopefully, alive.

"Well, look who's here," a throaty female voice came from behind him, and Sam sighed.

He knew that voice. Looked like his day was just going to get better and better. Surrendering to the inevitable, he turned around and dredged up a smile.

"Ma'am," he said, dipping his head into a slight nod.

"Ma'am?" Leeza Carter repeated with an indelicate snort of laughter. "Hell boy, we're practically family."

Oh, he wouldn't go that far, Sam thought. Leeza'd blown into the lives of the Fortune family when she'd come to San Antonio with Lloyd Wayne Carter. But then Lloyd, Miranda Fortune's ex-husband, tried to show off by riding a bronc in the rodeo and got himself killed. Everyone had figured Leeza would leave after that.

But she was as hard to get rid of as gum on the bottom of your shoe. And just about as appealing. Her bleached-blond hair looked as brittle as her washed-out lavender eyes, and she had a Mae West figure gone to seed. She'd spent most of her good years as a buckle bunny, following after rodeo riders. Now she was a bunny without a buckle.

"Doing some shopping, are you?" she asked, glancing from him to his still-empty cart.

"Yes ma'am, and I'd best get to it, if you'll excuse me." He didn't mean to be rude, but he sure as heck didn't have time to stand around and chat with a woman he didn't even like. Or wonder what that female was up to. And on that thought, he got back to the business at hand.

Trying to study the aisles and avoid collisions with other carts, he glanced up at the signs hanging from the ceiling. *Toiletries, paper goods, feminine hygiene.* Good Lord. Well that, at least, was one aisle he could skip.

Elevator music drifted out of the store speakers and every once in awhile, a voice cut into the music, shouting about a bargain to be had somewhere in the market. Kids whined and begged for prizes, mothers chatted in the aisles. But Sam hardly heard any of it. Stoically, he searched for the aisle he needed while silently trying to figure out how in the hell he'd gotten himself into this.

Michelle Guillaire parked her cart and studied the array of bakery goods, trying to decide if she'd been on her diet long enough. "After all," she murmured, "all veggies and no sugar makes Michelle a grumpy girl." She smiled to herself and reached for a box of chocolate donuts.

There was probably something twisted about re-

warding yourself for having lost five pounds by buy-
ing junk food, but she was too hungry to care. Tear-
ing the box open, she pulled out a donut and
munched on it as she wandered through the rest of
her shopping.

It felt good to be out and among people again.
She'd been spending way too much time lately
cooped up in her office with only the computer for
company. She smiled at a little girl busily tugging
unnoticed at her mother's jacket and tried to ignore
the soft pang around the edges of her own heart.
She'd always wanted children of her own.

Yet here she was, thirty-one years old and alone
as that poor, befuddled-looking soldier.

Michelle stopped, frowned to herself and backed
up, giving herself a good look at the man in uniform.
Her heart did a weird little two-step as her gaze
locked on him.

Tall, she thought, his light-brown hair trimmed
into a high and tight Marine haircut. She studied the
line of his jaw, the width of his shoulders, the length
of his legs. She knew the deep-green brilliance of his
eyes and the tenderness of his hands. Oh wow.

It was ten years since the last time he'd touched
her and yet, her skin was humming. Michelle took a
long, deep breath and told herself that they were
grownups. Adults. They could be friends. A sudden
rush of heat poured through her, putting the lie to
that idea.

Ridiculous, she thought and swallowed the last of her donut. She ran her tongue across her front teeth, checking for stray bits of chocolate, then self-consciously patted her hair and smoothed one hand down the front of her bloodred sweatshirt. Wouldn't you know she'd see him when she wasn't wearing makeup? Maybe she should just leave quickly, quietly. Pretend she hadn't seen him. But that wouldn't work. Her feet were already taking her toward him.

Michelle's mind raced in tandem with her heart. She'd heard Sam was back in town. She just hadn't planned on running into him at the grocery store, let alone in the…she looked around. *Baby food aisle?*

As she got closer, she heard him talking to himself and the sound of his deep, gruff voice sent splinters of awareness sparkling through her. Snatches of memory shot through her mind at lightning speed. The two of them, cuddled together in the darkness. His whisper rumbling along her spine as his hands moved over the rest of her.

Michelle frowned to herself and wondered why the grocery store was so darned hot.

"Strained carrots, strained spinach. They really expect kids to eat this stuff?" he asked aloud of no one.

"It's hard to gnaw on a good steak when you don't have teeth," Michelle quipped and braced herself, waiting for his reaction.

He went completely still for a long moment then

turned around slowly to face her. The minute those deep-green eyes of his locked with hers, Michelle felt her knees liquefy. Oh for heaven's sake. It was just like old times.

"Michelle."

No warm welcome in *that* voice, she thought, but at least he hadn't snarled at her. She swallowed hard, forced a smile and said, "Hi, Sam. I heard you were back in town." In fact, the minute he'd moved back to San Antonio, it seemed everyone she knew had made sure she heard about it.

His hands closed tightly on the two jars of baby food he held and she noticed his knuckles whitening. "Yeah. Been back about a month now."

Oh, this was going well.

"You look…" she paused, just managing to stop herself from saying something stupid like, *amazing*. "Good," she finished lamely, knowing it for the understatement of the century.

"You, too," he said, letting his gaze sweep over her and Michelle would have bet that she could actually *feel* her temperature rising.

"*Excuse* me," a woman said from behind her and Michelle jumped, moving her cart to one side of the aisle. She glanced at the older woman in the ugly pink hat and idly wondered why she gave Sam a dirty look as she marched past. But in the next instant, she dismissed the thought and asked, "So, what are you up to?"

"My neck," he said darkly, "and sinkin' fast."

"What?"

"Look at this," he said, holding up the jars of baby food and waving his right hand at the shelf in front of him. "How're you supposed to know what to get? What kind of vegetables? What brand? Jars or packages? Cereal or formula?" His voice inched up a notch higher as he went on. "And if it's formula, what kind? Soy? Liquid? Powder? Ready to drink? Mixable?"

Her lips twitched. "I thought you liked beer."

His gaze snapped to hers. "I do. And right now, I could use one."

Michelle thought she detected a glimmer of panic in his eyes, but that had to be a mistake. Nothing and no one scared Sam "Storm" Pearce. He hadn't earned that nickname by being a softie.

"What's going on, Sam?" she asked, and told herself it was simple curiosity that had prompted the question.

"Oh nothing," he muttered, gingerly setting the jars of food back onto the shelf, as if half expecting them all to come tumbling down in a baby-food avalanche. "Just the end of the world as I know it."

"Thought that happened last March."

"What?"

She shrugged. "I saw the article in the newspaper. You know…about you being one of the Fortunes?" She could only imagine how weird finding out that he was a member of an illustrious family had been for him.

Sam shifted position and his scowl darkened. "That's got nothing to do with this. That's…" He shook his head. "Hell, I'm not sure what that means yet."

Okay, she thought, his problem had nothing to do with him suddenly inheriting not only wealth, but an extended family. So what else could it be?

"Sounds serious."

"Damn straight."

Well, she thought. He was as talkative as ever. She used to tease him by saying that if he was ever captured by the enemy, any secrets he carried would be safe. Not even the threat of torture could coax more than one or two sentences out of him at a time.

He folded his arms across his chest, planted his feet wide apart in an "I dare you" posture and blurted, "I just became a father."

Stunned, Michelle just looked at him. This piece of news she hadn't been expecting. She hadn't heard anything about Sam having a wife. A twinge of regret poked at her insides as she tried to imagine the woman he'd created a child with. Well, what had she thought? That after she dumped him ten years ago, he'd entered a monastery? She'd moved on. Had a life. Why shouldn't Sam have done the same thing?

"I…" she said, searching for the right thing to say. By the look on his face, she was guessing congratulations weren't in order. Finally, she shrugged and said, *"Mazel tov?"*

He gave her a tight smile. "Thanks."

"Boy or girl?" she forced herself to ask.

"Twin girls."

Twins. Imagining two babies with his brilliant-green eyes, she strangled a little sigh of pure envy. "So, when did this happen?"

"A couple hours ago."

"Are you serious?" she asked. "Shouldn't you be at the hospital with your wife?"

"Huh?" Sam gave her a look, then shook his head. "I'm not married. You don't understand. The twins aren't newborns. These babies are nine months old."

Another cart rattled down the aisle and a harried-looking young woman excused herself, stepped between Michelle and Sam and snatched two cans of formula off the shelf. A moment later, they were alone again, listening to the bored voice of an announcer talking about the special the store was running on ground beef.

"I'm confused," Michelle said.

"Join the club," Sam muttered, then threw a glance down toward the far end of the aisle at the veritable mountain of disposable diapers. "Oh, man..."

"What's going on?" she prodded, more curious than ever.

Sam turned his gaze back to her. Truth to tell, he'd much rather look at Michelle anyway. Damn. Ten years had only improved her. The big red sweatshirt she wore disguised her figure, but the worn jeans hugging her shapely legs told him it hadn't changed much. Night-black hair framed her heart-shaped face before falling across her shoulders in thick, soft waves and her violet eyes shone with concern and curiosity.

He smiled to himself, remembering Michelle's curious streak, and how many times she'd told him that curiosity might have killed the cat, but at least it'd died informed.

Damned if he hadn't missed her. Oh, he hadn't wanted to. Hadn't planned on it. After all, when a woman turns down your marriage proposal, the natural instinct is to forget her just as fast as humanly possible.

Unfortunately, forgetting Michelle Guillaire was easier said than done.

"Sam?" she asked, dragging him back from thoughts too dangerous to consider anyway. "Are you going to tell me what's up or not?"

Hell, he hardly knew what was going on himself. He scraped one hand across his jaw, looked her dead in the eye and silently acknowledged that he needed a little help here. Why not get it from Michelle?

"The babies are my goddaughters. Their folks died in a scuba-diving accident a few days ago and in a few hours, I'm flying to Hawaii to pick them up."

"You have custody?" she asked quietly.

He couldn't blame her for being surprised. Hell, he was still in a state of shock himself. When Dave had asked him to be the kids' legal guardian, he'd agreed, never thinking that he'd actually be called on to do the job. But it appeared that Fate had a sense of humor.

"Just call me Sergeant Mom."

Two

A couple of beats passed while the information registered. Michelle ached for the parents who would never see their children grow up, but even as she thought it, she realized that now wasn't the time for pity. Michelle surged into action a moment later. After all, he only had a couple of hours before leaving to pick up these poor babies. The least *she* could do was help him get ready, right?

"I'll get the baby food," she told him, taking charge. "You go down and pick up some diapers."

He inhaled sharply and blew it out again. "At the risk of sounding like an old movie...I don't know nothin' 'bout babies. What the hell size do I get?"

She wasn't entirely sure of that herself. An only child, she hadn't exactly been surrounded by children growing up. And though she had a few friends with children, she'd never really gotten into the specifics of diaper-sizing. "I don't know. How about large? If they're too big, you can always fold them to make them smaller. You can't really stretch a too-small plastic and paper diaper."

"Sounds reasonable," he said, and strode down the aisle like a man on a mission.

Which he was, she thought, her gaze straying back to the shelves full of baby food. At least the makers were thoughtful enough to give age listings on the different jars. She picked out vegetables, meats and fruits along with juices and cereal. By the time she was finished, Sam was back and tossing a couple of packages of diapers into the cart.

"What else?" he asked.

"Milk," she told him. "Babies that old aren't drinking formula anymore."

"Thank God," he muttered. "Milk I can find."

She kept her cart right behind his as he headed for the dairy section. And on the way, she had the opportunity to admire his behind. Sam had always had one great butt.

"Regular?"

"Hmm?" She lifted her gaze quickly, like a teenager caught with a steamy book. "Oh, yeah. Regular's fine."

"Think that's it?" he asked, scanning the contents of the cart.

"For now," she said gruffly, then cleared her throat. "Is your apartment ready for them?"

"They're coming with only a diaper bag. I bought beds for them already if that's what you mean. They'll be delivered when I get back.

"That's part of it."

"What else is there?" he asked as if dreading to hear the answer. "They've got food and a place to sleep. What's left?"

"Lots of things," she told him and started to launch into a list when another thought occurred to her. "Look Sam, why don't I just go back to your place with you and help you get set up?"

His features tightened, and, for a moment, Michelle thought he might refuse her. And maybe that would be for the best, she thought. Being alone with Sam Pearce in his apartment probably wasn't such a good idea. It had been ten years, but judging by the trip-hammer rhythm of her heartbeat, their time apart hadn't been long enough to curb the kind of desire they'd had for each other.

Of course, he didn't look like he was having much problem keeping himself from lunging for her. So maybe this was all in her mind. Regret. It was bound to rear its ugly head from time to time, she supposed. And when faced with the man you'd once loved with every breath, it was only natural to get a little...all right, *a lot,* flustered.

But she wasn't the same girl she had been so many years ago. She'd changed. Grown up. She'd been married. She'd been widowed. Surely Sam had done some changing as well. What she was feeling was no doubt just the lingering embers from a love burned out years ago. Her reaction to him was probably along the lines of Pavlov's dogs. See Sam. Start drooling.

She could deal with this. She could prove to both of them that she'd done the right thing when she'd broken up with him so long ago.

Since he still hadn't spoken, Michelle said, "Look, you said yourself you've only got a couple of hours before you have to leave. If I help, you'll get done in half the time."

He considered that for a half a minute and finally nodded abruptly. "Okay," he said. "I appreciate the offer."

Michelle plastered a too-wide smile on her face and asked, "What are friends for?"

"Is that what we are?" Sam wondered aloud. *"Friends?"*

"We could be," she said softly. "And it's better than enemies, right?"

"I was never your enemy, Michelle," he told her and his voice was soft and rough, scraping like sandpaper along her spine.

"I know that," she said, "it's just—"

"Look," he interrupted. "It'd probably be easier all the way around if we didn't talk about the past. Why don't we just start over. Fresh. From here."

"All right," she said, and stepped to one side as he pushed his cart past her, headed for the checkout aisles at the front of the store.

But as she followed after him, Michelle told herself that just because they weren't going to *talk* about their past didn't mean that they both weren't *thinking* about it.

His "apartment" was actually a tiny house set far back on a wide, deep lot. Several ancient oak trees shaded the front yard and there was a rope hammock strung between the two trees closest to the front porch. The old wood-frame house was in need of a paint job, but somehow the faded white paint and black shutters only gave it a more comfortable, lived-in look than its spick-and-span modernized neighbors.

A few late blooming chrysanthemum bushes straggled in their beds along the driveway, making tattered splotches of color against the less-than-perfect lawn. And as Michelle parked her car behind Sam's, a part of her mind was already busily tending the flowers, mowing the grass and giving the place a little TLC.

Honestly, she had to curb this nesting instinct. Especially with Sam. Not only wasn't it warranted, but she was fairly certain it wouldn't be appreciated, either.

But she couldn't seem to help herself. After all, she planned events for a living. Weddings especially. And a yard like this would be perfect for a party. Plenty of room for guests to wander around. She could almost see the tables and chairs scattered across the grass, white tablecloths fluttering in a soft breeze. There would be paper lanterns strung from the branches of the trees and tiny white lights twinkling high in the foliage. Without even trying, she could practically hear the soft muted conversations and the clink of crystal glassware. Yep. Sam's front yard would be a perfect party spot with a little work. And it was in her nature to see something and try to fix it up.

"You coming?" Sam called, and she tore her gaze from the faded glory of his yard to look at him standing beside the trunk of his car.

"Yeah," she said, grabbing her purse off the seat and opening the door.

It was a lovely afternoon. But then, January in Texas is occasionally pretty wonderful. It was days like this that reminded the citizens of Texas just why they loved the place so much. A sky so blue it almost hurt to look at it stretched out overhead, and a slight breeze ruffled Michelle's hair as she walked toward Sam.

He tossed her his keys, picked up the bags of supplies out of the trunk and nodded for her to slam the lid back down. When she had, he started for the front door and paused on the bottom step to let her past him.

Michelle jammed the key home, turned it in the lock, then opened the door to a typical bachelor's house. The hardwood floor was dotted with discarded socks and underwear. A stack of newspapers teetered dangerously on a chair somehow balanced on three legs, and the scent of fried bacon mixed with cigarette smoke hung in the still air.

She sniffed and turned to him. "I thought you quit smoking ten years ago."

"Did," he said, marching past her toward a door at the far end of the room. "Poker game last night."

Which explained the empty beer bottles and crumpled bags of potato-chip crumbs scattered across the top of the pedestal table.

Oh, yeah. He was in great shape to bring babies home. Just glancing around the room, she noted a few glaringly unsafe baby spots. Shaking her head, she followed after him and stepped into a kitchen that was probably considered "state of the art" when it was built…around 1930.

Sky-blue tile edged with a navy-blue border lined the long countertop and the single sink was deep enough for the washing machine to empty into. An impossibly small refrigerator sat huddled in a corner beside a stove that looked old enough to be a wood-burner. On the far wall, a built-in corner cabinet, meant to hold china, now boasted a supply of paper plates and colorful plastic glasses. The tiny table beneath the wide front window still held a plate of petrifying egg yolk and half a slice of bacon…remnants, no doubt, of Sam's breakfast.

She did a slow turn, taking in the long, narrow room before looking at him and saying, "Nice place you've got here."

He paused in emptying the bags and gave her a quick look. "I wasn't expecting company."

"But you *are* expecting babies."

"Yeah? So?"

"*So,*" Michelle said as she grabbed baby food and searched for a cupboard to store it in, "this place is nowhere near baby-proofed." She stared open-mouthed into the cupboard, dazed at the collection of potato-chip bags and canned soup. Is this all he ate? Shaking her head, she cleared off one shelf and systematically started stacking jars of strained fruits and vegetables.

"What do you mean baby-proofed?"

"I mean things like all of the cords you've got stretched across the living-room floor. The cable box, the glass-topped coffee table, the three-legged chair just primed to fall over onto a crawling infant."

He scowled to himself and tossed the empty bag toward the trash can. "I just found out about Dave and Jackie's accident a couple of hours ago,'' he said. ''There hasn't been time to—'' He stopped talking, looked at her and admitted, ''Hell. Even if I'd had a week, I wouldn't have thought about baby-proofing the place.'' Clearly disgusted, he muttered, ''Oh, yeah. This is gonna work out great.''

''It's not that bad,'' Michelle said and carefully folded the empty bag before going to retrieve the one on the floor. As she smoothed it flat, she continued, ''I mean, you could have the place ready in a day or two. It just takes a little planning.''

''I don't have a day or two,'' Sam told her and checked his watch. ''I don't even have two hours, now.''

He was in a bind. A tight one. And Michelle's instinct was to jump in and fix everything. Maybe she'd regret it later, but for right now, she just couldn't keep herself from suggesting, ''Why don't you leave me your key, and I'll get the place ready while you're gone?''

''What?''

''Sure,'' she said, obviously on a roll. ''The store could deliver the cribs, and I could have them all set up and everything else ready by the time you get back.''

Sam stared at her for a long minute, not really sure if he'd heard her right. He hadn't spoken to her in a decade and the last time they *had* talked, they hadn't exactly left things on a friendly note. And now she was volunteering to dig him out of this hole he found himself in?

Why?

"I mean it," she was saying, already moving around the kitchen, picking things up, straightening, stacking dishes into the sink and running water on them. "In a week I could have this place ready for the babies."

"I'm sure you could," he said, and wondered if his voice sounded as tight to her as it did to him. "The question is, why do you want to?"

She stilled, then slowly reached for the water faucet and turned it off. The sudden quiet strained the air between them until she turned to look at him. Giving him a half smile that in the old days had never failed to kick-start his heart, she said simply, "Let's call it helping out a friend."

Friends.

The one thing he'd never felt for Michelle had been friendship. He'd wanted her. Loved her. Lusted after her until he couldn't think beyond the next opportunity to touch her. And when she'd turned down his marriage proposal, he'd come close to hating her. But he'd never wanted to be her friend.

"This is pity, right?" he asked.

She pulled her head back and stared at him. "Pity?"

"Yeah. You figure I can't handle this so you'll ride to the rescue?"

Michelle blinked at him, reached for a crumpled dish towel and dried her hands. "I didn't mean to offend you. I was only trying to help."

Damn it. Sam shoved one hand across the top of his head, glanced down at his wristwatch and felt the seconds ticking past. He hadn't meant to snarl at her. But then he hadn't expected to run into her, stirring up old feelings better left buried. But was it *her* fault that he hadn't been able to let go of the past?

No.

Did he need her help, whatever had prompted her offer?

Oh, yeah.

She moved past him, headed for the doorway and he reached out, grabbing her arm, stopping her. A scattering of heat erupted in the middle of his chest like a shotgun blast. He released her instantly, but it wasn't quick enough.

"Michelle," he said, shoving his hands into his pockets, "look, I didn't mean to be a jerk."

"You weren't."

"Yeah I was," he said, then added, "but I don't even have time to apologize. So if you really meant it—about offering to help—I'd…appreciate it."

She smiled then and it nearly knocked his socks off. Damn it. It didn't seem fair that he could still be so affected by this one woman. This probably wasn't a good idea, he told himself, already realizing that too much time spent with her could only cause them both grief. But on the other hand, he was in no position to turn down help when it was so desperately needed.

He supposed he could go to the Fortune family and ask for assistance. But those relationships were still so new, so tenuous, that he didn't feel right about it. Nope. If there was help coming his way, it would be coming from Michelle.

"Good," she said, then asked, "so, how are you getting to the airport?"

"I'll drive myself, leave the car in long-term parking."

She shook her head already moving for the door. "No need for that," she said. "I'll take you. And pick you up. You'll need help with the babies."

Oh, he had no doubt she'd be a big help with the babies. But, he wondered, as he picked up his duffle bag and stepped out of the house to follow her to her car, just who in the hell was going to help him with Michelle?

Swarms of people surrounded them and streamed past like schools of fish heading for food. As the last call sounded for his flight, Michelle summoned up a wide smile. "Good luck. Now, you've got my phone number. Call me when you're sure of your return flight."

"I will," he said, and cast a glance at the dwindling line of passengers boarding the plane. "I've got to go."

Michelle nodded, and, before she knew what she was doing, she reached for him and gave him a hug. Stunned surprise rippled through her at her own actions. Lord, what must he be thinking? she wondered.

But a moment later, she had her answer. His arms snaked around her and squeezed her briefly, tightly. Then he released her, and, in a second or two, he was gone.

And Michelle, as always, was alone.

Three

Sam had never been on a trip that seemed as long as this one. Hell, flying military transport to the Persian Gulf paled in comparison.

Three days later, a long line of people now snaked along the center aisle of the plane. Frustrated mutters whispered through the cabin as tired passengers shifted from foot to foot, waiting for their fellow travelers to unload carry-on baggage from the overhead compartments.

Sam sympathized. Carry-on bags used to mean one small suitcase. Now it included laptops, guitars, strollers, garment bags... He'd never understood why people had to drag every piece of luggage they owned with them into the cabin. Hell, after flying for five or six hours, what was another fifteen-minute wait at the baggage carousel?

A whimpering half cry sounded from just beside Sam, and he turned his head to look at one of the twins. He couldn't tell them apart, but he'd already given them nicknames. This one was "the Crier." The slightest thing would set her off. Her sister on the other hand, was "the Spitter," which sounded kinder than "the Puker." She'd earned that name in the first five minutes of their acquaintance when she'd lost her lunch, literally, down the front of Sam's uniform.

The Crier and the Spitter both had howled most of the way from Hawaii. If not for the flight attendants' help, he was pretty sure his fellow passengers would have tossed him *and* the babies out the nearest airlock. He reached up and scraped both hands across his face. Sam felt as if he'd been in a hot zone for hours with no relief. Only instead of bullets, there'd been bottles and dirty diapers and screeching that had only occasionally faded into a wail.

Reaching for the Crier, Sam lifted her out of the infant seat and set her on his lap. One big hand against her back to steady her, they stared at each other.

"Look," he said quietly, "I know I'm not real good at this, but you might consider giving me a break."

The baby sucked in her lower lip, and a single tear escaped the corner of her eye. It rolled down her plump cheek and disappeared into the folds on her neck. Sam's heart twisted in his chest.

She didn't deserve him. Neither of the babies did. They deserved what all kids did. A good home and parents who loved them. Everything they'd had until just a week ago, he reminded himself. And not for the first time, he wondered what the girls were thinking, feeling. Did they know their parents were gone, never to return? Were they scared of all the new faces in their lives? Could they tell just how lost Sam felt?

Man, he hoped not.

From the corner of his eye, he noticed movement. As if someone had opened a gate somewhere, the line of people in the aisle suddenly started making some headway. One after another left the plane, and Sam started gathering up babies and the gear they'd required. Before he could stand up though, an older man wearing a rumpled suit and a nasty disposition stopped alongside his seat.

"You know, you and your children ruined this flight. I've never heard such a noise," the man snapped, glaring first at Sam, then at each of the babies.

He'd been thinking the same thing a few minutes ago, but hearing this guy say it was something else again. "Sir," Sam said, giving the man the look he gave slow recruits on the drill field, "everybody on board this plane started off as babies. Even you. And we all cried. We all irritated some old goat."

"Old goat?" the man repeated, obviously insulted.

The Crier actually giggled, a deep, throaty laugh that seemed to bubble up from her stomach. Sam gave her a quick smile, then returned his gaze to the man still standing as if rooted to the spot. *"And,"* he continued his defense of the babies, "these two girls have got a hell of a lot more reason to complain than you do. They just lost their parents in an accident. They've been ripped out of their home, taken from everything familiar, thrown onto a plane with a stranger and you expect them to be *quiet?* Mister, if all that had happened to you, I suspect you'd be making a good bit of noise yourself."

The man had the good manners to look a bit ashamed of himself before clearing his throat and huffing off down the aisle. A woman just behind him paused long enough to give Sam a grin and a whispered, "Bravo!"

Then the last of the passengers were gone, and Sam was left with the girls who had, overnight, become his daughters.

God help them both.

Michelle heard them before she saw them. A whimper drifted up through the long disembarking tunnel, and she was already moving toward it when

Sam walked into view. A baby girl on each arm, he also carried a brightly flowered diaper bag slung over his shoulder. He had the look of a man standing at the edge of a cliff wondering if jumping was really such a bad idea.

Her earlier doubts about whether it was wise to get re-involved with Sam disappeared under a surprisingly strong tidal wave of maternal instinct. One look at those two faces…so much alike…so heart-breakingly innocent, and she was a dead duck.

Hurrying up to them, Michelle held out her arms and one of the babies flung itself at her. "Oh, you poor thing," Michelle murmured as the infant cuddled close, sniffing and whimpering.

Sam sighed heavily and said, "I don't think I've ever been so glad to see anybody in my life."

A brief thrill of pleasure scuttled through her before Michelle could stop it. But, an instant later, she realized he would have been just as happy to see a matronly woman of eighty if she'd been willing to help him with the babies.

She swallowed back a knot of disappointment, telling herself that it was just as well. She didn't *want* him to want her, after all. "Rough flight?" she asked.

"You don't even want to know," he grumbled and hitched the baby in his arms a bit higher.

Michelle ran one hand up and down the baby's back, automatically soothing the child while at the same time studying Sam's features. He looked tired. Still, they were such sweet babies. "Oh, come on," she said, cocking her head to one side. "You mean to tell me a big, strong Marine can't handle a couple of baby girls?"

Sam shook his head. "I would rather go back to the Persian Gulf. Alone. Armed only with a BB gun—than go through another flight like that one."

A smile twitched her lips, but when his eyes narrowed, she let the smile fade as she nodded. "Right then. Maybe we'd better get you guys home."

"God, that sounds good," he said on a half groan. Turning, he started walking with the crowd toward baggage claim and shot Michelle a quick glance as she hurried to keep pace with him. "You have no idea how much I've been thinking about getting back to my place and just relaxing."

"I can imagine," she said, loving the feel of the small warm body cuddled close to her chest. The little girl wriggled a bit, buried her face in the curve of Michelle's neck, and it was all she could do not to sigh in satisfaction.

Good heavens, this maternal thing was stronger than she'd ever thought. She hadn't known this baby more than five minutes, and here she was cuddling and cooing and falling hopelessly in love. This wasn't good, she thought, silently reminding herself that these babies weren't hers. Heck, they weren't even hers to visit. She was only here to help. Then she'd be fading into the background. Disappearing from Sam's life...*again*.

But somehow, all of the logic in the world wasn't strong enough to compete with the emotions racing through her. She wanted to hold these girls. Love them. Try to make up to them what they'd lost. And to enjoy what she'd never be able to have.

"Are you listening?" Sam asked, and Michelle was jerked out of her thoughts to stare at him and say, "What?"

He shook his head and gave her a ghost of a smile. "Off daydreaming again, huh?"

"Sort of," she admitted, though he'd have to tie her down atop a Fire Ant hill to get her to tell him what her daydream had been about.

The hustle and bustle of the busy airport terminal seemed to dissolve as he looked into her eyes, and Michelle felt herself falling forward into those familiar green depths. Oh, boy.

"Some things never change, do they?"

"What do you mean?" she asked, and almost tripped over her own feet before she had the presence of mind to tear her gaze from his.

"I mean, you used to zone out all the time."

"Zone out?"

"Yeah," Sam said, and one corner of his mouth tilted into a half smile. "We'd be talking about one thing, and I'd notice your eyes go all soft and dreamy. Before I knew it, you were off in the atmosphere somewhere.''

She didn't know quite what to say to that, so she kept quiet. Which is the only reason she heard him murmur, ''I missed that, for a long time.''

Her throat closed, and a knot formed in the pit of her stomach. She'd missed him, too. It hadn't been easy to say no to Sam's proposal. In fact, watching him walk away from her was the hardest thing she'd ever done. But she'd been so sure she was doing the right thing. For both of them.

Then a year or so later, she'd married William. Oh, she hadn't loved him as she'd loved Sam, but he'd been a kind, good man. And when he died only two years into their marriage, Michelle had taken back her maiden name and put all thoughts of family out of her mind. Some people, she'd told herself, just weren't destined to be part of a family.

Although now, ten years after losing Sam, she wasn't sure of anything anymore.

Echoes of memories clung to them both as they made their way down to baggage claim. By the time they arrived, most of the luggage had been claimed and Sam's Marine-green duffel bag was practically alone on the carousel. He reached for it as it sailed past, and the diaper bag on his shoulder swung forward and slapped him in the face.

Michelle said, ''Give me that,'' and reached for the yellow-and-orange flowered bag.

"It's heavy," he warned as he handed it over.

"I'm a big girl," she told him.

"Yeah," he muttered thickly, deliberately looking away from her. "So I've noticed."

Then with each of them carrying one bag and one baby, they headed for the parking lot and Sam's car.

The wide, tree-shaded street seemed to welcome him home. The sun was easing its way down the sky as he pulled into the driveway and stopped. A week, Sam told himself. He'd been gone only one short week, and he hardly recognized the place.

The flowers alongside the drive had been cut back. The grass had been mowed and the shrubs trimmed. A pair of wicker chairs he'd had stuffed into the garage had been painted white and plunked down on the front porch where they waited for someone to come and sit awhile. Pots of ivy hung from the rafters over the porch.

He should have been expecting this. Michelle never had been one for sitting still. Give the woman ten minutes and a paint brush and she could touch up the Sistine Chapel.

Sam shook his head, then slowly, turned to look at her. "You've been busy," he said dryly.

"Well," she said, waving one hand toward the house while keeping her gaze locked with his, "I just thought—"

"The house needed help as much as I did?" he finished for her.

"I didn't mean anything by it," she said defensively. "I just straightened up a few things."

"And painted, and planted and...what the hell else, Michelle?"

Her lips tightened, and he recognized the flash of impatience in her eyes. Time, it seemed, hadn't done a thing toward calming the temper that was always close to the surface.

"Look," she ground out as she opened her car door, "if you don't like it, change it back."

He reached out and grabbed her upper arm before she could slide out of the car. Heat sizzled through him and this time, he didn't let her go. This time, he let himself enjoy the wave of pleasure that came simply from touching her. It had been so long. *Too* long, since he'd felt anything like it.

He'd tried to lose himself in other women. Tried to recapture what he'd found in Michelle. But it had always eluded him. No one affected him as she did.

Man, how he used to love to touch her. Her hand, her face, her hair. He remembered all too well the feel of her curves beneath his palms. The soft, hitching breath she'd take when he entered her body. Watching her, loving her, holding her had been all he'd ever wanted. And then he'd made the mistake of proposing, and she'd shot him out of the sky with one well-aimed missile.

Well, he thought as a coldness settled over the fire inside, smothering it, so much for memories.

He released her and opened his own car door. But before getting out, he said gruffly, "I didn't say I didn't like it."

"What exactly did you say then?" she asked as she stepped out of the car. Leaning one forearm on the roof of the small black sedan, she stared at him, waiting.

"All I said was, you'd been busy," Sam repeated and stared back at her. "Nobody expected you to do any of this, Michelle. You said you were going to get things ready for the babies. That's all."

Her expression shifted from defensive to embarrassment in a heartbeat. Then shrugging, she said, "I did. But then I had a little more time and I—" She broke off and sighed. Reaching up, she pushed one hand through her thick black hair impatiently. "I'm sorry. I got a little…carried away."

Sam's fingers itched to spear through her soft, silky hair. He wanted to feel it against his skin again. And because that want was so sharp, so desperate, he wanted to make *her* feel it, too. "Carried away, huh? Now where have I heard that before?"

As he'd hoped, memory dawned instantly on her features. He watched a slow flush of color spread up her neck and into her cheeks. She straightened up away from the car and looked everywhere but at him.

"*Now* I remember," Sam said, pretending to

dredge up a long-ignored recollection, when, in reality, he'd have to be dead fifty years before forgetting anything about his time with Michelle.

"We were in the back row of the movie house…"

"Sam…" She shot him a suddenly panicked look and plucked a long strand of wind-tossed hair from in front of her eyes.

He saw the plea in her gaze. He knew she wanted him to be quiet. And maybe that was part of the reason he couldn't. He'd had ten years of quiet. Ten years of keeping his memories to himself. Well, enough was enough. Let her know. Let her realize that he remembered it all.

"It was one of those middle-of-the-night showings of an old black-and-white movie from the thirties…" He nodded and stared off into space, seeing it all, feeling it all again, as he had so many times over the years. The quiet neighborhood fell away and once again he was in the dark theatre, kissing Michelle. "We had the whole place to ourselves and—"

"We really ought to get the girls inside, don't you think?" Michelle asked, her voice tight, hurried.

"Light and shadows flickered on your face," he mused. "Don't know why we paid to see that movie. We didn't watch it."

"Sam…" Michelle said and her voice was even tighter now, thicker. He heard the echo of his own hunger ringing in her tone. But he couldn't stop now. In truth, didn't *want* to stop.

He met her gaze squarely, and the violet of her eyes seemed to be on fire. His chest tightened. His heart thudded painfully, and still he kept talking. He needed to make her remember. Needed to know if the memories could scorch her as hotly as they did him. Needed to know that she hadn't walked away from him without suffering.

He turned his face into the cool wind, but it did nothing to quench the fires within. "I had to touch you. Had to feel your skin on mine."

Her eyes closed briefly, and she swayed against the car. "Don't do this," she murmured. "Don't do this to either one of us." But it was a faint request. He saw her breath hitch. Watched the pulse-beat at the base of her throat quicken. Then she opened her eyes again, and, holding her gaze, Sam went on.

"But you needed me, too, Michelle. Remember?"

She nodded jerkily. "I remember."

"There in the darkness," he said, "you climbed onto my lap."

"Sam, please…"

"And you took me inside you."

"Oh, no…" Her palms flattened atop the roof of the car, and she swallowed hard as the memory washed over her.

"We made love there, Michelle, in the flickering light. In that theater, alone in the shadows, you rode me until I could hardly breathe. Until I didn't care if

I could breathe or not. All I cared about was you. And being with you. Inside you.''

"Oh, my..."

Her eyes glazed over, and Sam's body tightened until he thought he might burst. She did remember. All of it.

"And when it was over," he said tightly, determined to finish this, "and we were leaning into each other, shaking, do you remember what you said?"

A long moment ticked past before she nodded and swallowed hard. Then, staring into his eyes, she whispered, "I said, 'Sorry, Sam. I guess I got a little carried away.'"

His insides twisted hard and tight, and he had to wonder just which of them he was punishing by opening up this particular can of worms. But it was too late now.

Four

Michelle took a long, deep breath and tried to ignore the stuttering beat of her heart. Her whole body felt flushed. Alive. Red-hot with remembered sensation and too darn eager to feel it all again.

Get a grip, she told herself silently. That was a long time ago. Things were different then. *She'd* been different then. Young, and so in love she couldn't see beyond their next night together, she hadn't worried or even *thought* about the future. Until he'd asked her to marry him. Have a family with him. And then—well, what was the point of rehashing all of this now?

She shifted position slightly and bent to take a quick peek at the babies in their car seats.

"They're still asleep," Sam said, dragging her attention back to him. "And even if they were awake, they wouldn't understand us."

"Why are you doing this?" she asked quietly and congratulated herself on the steadiness of her voice. Quite an accomplishment really, considering the fact that her entire body was trembling.

"Doing what?" he asked with a shrug.

"Cut it out," she snapped, shooting him a look that would have fried a lesser man. "You know darn well what you're doing."

"Kicking over some good times with an old 'friend?'"

Sam Pearce trying to look innocent was about as convincing as the Devil himself sporting a halo. This was ridiculous. She would not be dragged down memory lane. She would not apologize for what she'd done.

And she would not be embarrassed or regret anything she and Sam had done together out of love.

"Are you *trying* to hurt me?" she asked quietly, keeping her gaze locked on his.

"Hell no, I'm not trying to hurt you," he snapped and brushed one hand across the top of his head. His high and tight military haircut wasn't the slightest bit affected by the action.

"Then what?" she demanded. "What's the point of this?"

"Oh," he said, throwing his hands high, then letting them drop to his sides. "There has to be a *point*. Well, then, I guess the point is, I wanted you to remember."

"You think I don't?" she asked, dumbfounded. For heaven's sake, did he really believe she could have forgotten *anything* about their time together? Even marriage to another man hadn't wiped Sam from her mind, though she doubted he'd want to hear that.

"What am I supposed to think?" he muttered, leaning both forearms on the roof of the car. Folding his hands together, he stared at her. "You cut me loose ten years ago, despite everything we had going for us. Then, when we bump into each other, you're all 'let's be friends.' And I'm supposed to go along with it."

"*You're* the one who said we would start fresh," she reminded him, stabbing her index finger in the air for emphasis. "*You're* the one who didn't want to talk about the past."

"I changed my mind."

"Yeah, well, so did I." Stupid, stupid, stupid, she thought, closing her car door and moving for the back.

"Damn it, Michelle," he said.

Her head snapped up and she pinned him with a frosty glare. "Don't you curse at me. You don't have the right."

He inhaled sharply and blew it out again in a rush.

"Fine. You're right. I don't have the right. Just the *desire* to curse at you."

"Oh," she said with a nod of her head, "that's just lovely. Thank you so much. I feel so warm and cuddly now."

"What did you expect me to say?" he snapped, closing his own door and reaching for the handle to the back door. "'Gee, it's great to see you?' Or, how about, 'Want to rip my heart out again?'"

"All I expected was to help you with the babies."

"Why?"

"What?"

"I asked why." He paused and looked at her, watching the way the wind tossed her shoulder-length hair into a tangle of thick curls. It had been so long. He wondered if her hair still smelled like coconut, and then he told himself it didn't matter. *She* didn't matter. But even he didn't believe that one. "Fixing up my house, helping with the twins, why are you doing it? You never really answered me the last time I asked. Is it just for pity's sake? Not that I'm in a position to object, I'd just like to know."

"So would I," she said, so softly the wind almost carried her words away before he could catch them. Then she cleared her throat, met his gaze directly and asked, "Can't we just get the babies settled and leave it at that? Do we have to talk about this now?"

Hell yes, he wanted to shout. He wanted answers.

Not just to the question of why she was helping him now, but to the question of what had gone wrong between them so long ago. He wanted to know the reason she'd turned him away without so much as a backward glance. And the fact that that still bothered him irritated hell out of Sam.

He should be over it. It wasn't as if he'd joined a monastery after they'd broken up. Just the opposite, in fact. He'd hooked up with every woman he could find in a futile attempt to push thoughts of Michelle Guillaire out of his mind. He'd dated them, bedded them then forgotten them. Not one of them had ever come even close to getting under his skin the way Michelle had.

She'd opened the door to dreams of family, home and love…then she'd slammed that door in his face. An ache he'd thought long buried resurfaced suddenly and squeezed his heart until he nearly winced with the pain.

Sam had thought so many times of what he might say or do if he should ever run into her again. Strange that when he finally had, none of his well-thought-out plans had occurred to him.

That day in the grocery store, he'd been too panicked at the idea of preparing for the babies to actually be able to think about what seeing Michelle again was doing to him. But today, it had been a different story.

Stepping out of the boarding tunnel to find her

standing there waiting for him had fed fantasies he'd thought long forgotten. Back when he was younger and completely nuts about her, he'd imagined that very scene countless times. Him coming home from deployment. Michelle there on the base tarmac waiting for him. Smiling at him. Hungry for him. He'd even allowed himself to imagine a couple of kids who would have been dancing up and down in their excitement at seeing Daddy again.

And though today *he'd* been the one with the kids, it had been close enough to the fantasies that he'd had to stop himself from grabbing her and kissing her, losing himself in her until the years faded into the past and all they had left was the present. And the future.

"Sam?"

He blinked and looked at her. Really looked at her, not through the mirror of memory, but as she was now. Thinner than he remembered, with a few more lines at the corners of her violet eyes, she was even more beautiful now. And he wanted her more than his next breath.

But he could handle that. He was used to not getting what he wanted, wasn't he?

"No," he said, his voice thick with emotion he refused to recognize. "We don't have to talk about it."

Relief shone in her eyes, and, as she bent to free

one of the twins from her car seat, Sam added softly,
"Yet."

She'd been busy *inside* the house as well, Sam
thought, his gaze flicking around the once-familiar
rooms. Every piece of furniture had been polished to
such a high gleam, the late-afternoon sunshine pouring through the windows bounced off the wood sur-
faces and glittered brightly. Throw pillows had been
added to the couch, and the aroma of slow-cooked
chicken drifted out of the kitchen to slam into Sam's
empty stomach.

Following after Michelle, he felt like a visitor in
his own place. Obviously right at home in his house,
she led him into the spare room he'd been planning
on turning into a nursery. And on the threshold, he
stopped dead, amazed.

In three short days, she'd taken a spare room and
turned it into a children's fairyland world. The cribs
were assembled and set up like twin beds, so the girls
could see each other. In between the cribs was a
white table holding a Little Bo Peep lamp and two
or three storybooks. A small rocking chair sat beside
the table as if just waiting for a storyteller to make
himself comfortable.

The ceiling had been painted a soft sky blue and
dotted with white clouds. The sky theme was continued halfway down the walls, where she'd painted a
white picket fence. Red, yellow and orange flowers

peeked through the slats of the fence, making the room look like the outdoors, like the middle of a garden. There were two dressers, a changing table stocked with supplies and something called the Diaper Dragon hunched in a corner.

Just imagine, he told himself, what she could have done with the place if he'd given her a week.

Slowly, Sam turned to stare at her in open admiration. She looked nervous, as if waiting to see whether he'd thank her or be mad that she'd done too much.

"This is amazing," he said, stepping into the room and doing a slow turn, the better to admire her handiwork from all angles.

"You like it?" she asked, clearly relieved.

"What's not to like?" he asked, and set the Spitter down into one of the cribs. She immediately grabbed at the soft, stuffed lamb sitting on the mattress beside her and chewed on its ear. Of course she was hungry. She'd upchucked everything he'd fed her today. "You must have worked nonstop."

She shrugged as if dismissing all the hours she had to have put in on this room.

"You don't think it's too much?" Michelle asked, turning her head to study her paint job. "I guess I got a little carried—" she broke off instantly and shot him a look.

Something stirred inside him again, and Sam was forced to admit just how close to the surface his feelings for her still were. Damn it. He wouldn't let this happen. He would *not* go down this road one more time.

So, instead of making some smart-ass remark, he only said, "Thanks for all you did. I appreciate it."

Relief washed over her features as she took her cue from him and talked about anything but what still lay between them. "I was happy to," she said. "And if you want me to, I can stay awhile and help get them fed and down for the night."

He knew he should say no. Knew he should tell her to leave. Now. While he was still willing to let her go. But a part of him just wasn't ready to watch her walk out of his life again. Not just yet, anyway.

"That'd be good," he said.

And Michelle smiled at him. The force of that smile rocked him right down to the soles of his feet, and Sam knew instantly he'd made another mistake.

She turned to the baby she'd carried inside and bent over the top rail of the crib. Glancing at Sam over her shoulder, Michelle said, "You know, you never told me their names."

Sam tore his gaze away from the curve of her behind and told himself to stop going there. To stop torturing himself. Deliberately, he turned away from the picture she made bent over the Crier's crib. "Marie and Beth," he said.

"Which one's which?"

"You got me."

"What?" Michelle straightened up and whirled around to stare at him in disbelief. "You don't know one from the other?"

He glanced at her and said a bit defensively, "Well, look at 'em. Like two peas in one confusing pod."

Michelle looked from one baby to the other and back again. Soft black hair, dimples, big blue eyes. Okay, they were identical twins. But they each had their own identity, too. They weren't interchangeable. "Sam, you have to be able to tell them apart."

"Yeah, I know." He scowled a bit and admitted, "But I've got a system for that. At least for awhile."

"Really. And just what might that be?"

He straightened up, scraped one hand across the dark shadow of whiskers lining his jaw and said abruptly, "Take her shoes off."

Michelle just stared at him. "I beg your pardon."

"The Crier's shoes. Take 'em off."

"You call her the Crier?"

"Appropriate," he said as the baby in question started winding up for another howling jag, "don't you think?"

Michelle reached into the crib and absently patted the baby's behind. "And what do you call the other one?"

"The Spitter."

"Sam!" Appalled, Michelle looked at the sweet-faced baby in the crib opposite her.

"If you could see what she did to my uniform, you'd understand the name. Look," Sam said when she kept looking at him as if he ought to be lined up against the nearest wall and shot, "I'm new at this, all right? If you want to know their real names, take their shoes off."

Muttering under her breath about Neanderthal men and their ridiculous answers to life's little riddles, Michelle leaned over the crib again and quickly untied the tiniest set of sneakers she'd ever seen. As she slid them off, the baby kicked her feet in delight, making Michelle work double-time to catch those feet long enough to tug off the ruffled pink socks, too.

As soon as she did, though, she stared at the soles of those tiny feet in mute fascination. Shaking her head, she told herself she had to admire the man's ingenuity, even if she didn't agree with what he'd done.

"So," Sam asked, "which one do you have?"

Michelle caught one little foot and read off the name that had been printed in black marker along the sole. "This is Beth."

"Ah," he said, glancing at the Spitter. "So you're Marie."

A helpless chuckle escaped Michelle as she said, "I can't believe you wrote on their feet."

"Well, how else was I going to remember who was who?"

"Oh, I don't know, look at their faces maybe? Find the subtle differences that make them who they are?"

"Easy for you to say," Sam grumbled and started undressing little Marie. "I blew into Hawaii, had meetings with Social Services, then went to the County Home where they gave me fifteen minutes worth of instructions, a diaper bag, and sent me on my way. There wasn't a whole lot of time for 'subtle differences.'"

"But writing on their feet?" Michelle shook her head, appalled and yet fascinated by his solution to a problem.

"The County had name tags pinned to their chests," he muttered. "Like they were refugees waiting to go through Ellis Island or something. I thought this was better. At least no one would see their feet but me."

A soft, gentle squeeze around her heart brought a sheen of moisture to Michelle's eyes. Sam Pearce might talk like a tough guy, but his heart was a marshmallow. And whether he knew it or not, these babies had already landed him, hook, line and sinker.

So writing on their feet was a little…unusual. He'd found a way to protect their separate identities and keep them from being the object of well-meant pity from strangers. And he would continue to care for them long after the black marker had faded away.

Michelle had always known he'd be a wonderful

father. Even ten years ago, when they were both so young, she'd felt it instinctively. She still remembered all the long talks they'd had, how he'd told her about the houseful of children he wanted one day. And what good times they'd have together. He was a man who had hungered for family. And now, he finally had it. Not only was he a member of one of the most powerful families in the state—the Fortunes—now he was a father, as well.

And Michelle had no part in his—or their—life.

Nothing that is, beyond her new role of helpful friend. But would that be enough? Could it be enough? For either of them?

With the babies bathed, fed and put to bed, the old house settled down like a well-satisfied matron. The foundation creaked and groaned as it prepared for night and the sounds were cozy, comforting to the two people sitting on the sofa.

She should have left an hour ago, Michelle thought. But she hadn't. Instead, she'd had dinner with him, there in his little dining room, and they'd talked like two people very carefully dancing around the one issue haunting them both. Now, with the dishes done and the house quiet, she knew she should grab her purse and make a run for it. But somehow, she couldn't quite bring herself to say goodbye yet. Once she left, she wouldn't have a reason to come back. After all, these babies weren't *her* responsibility. She had no claim to them. No right to come around and hold them, play with them.

Just as she had no right to be near Sam anymore. She watched him as he bent over the hearth, building a small fire to ward off the January chill in the air. His hands, capable and strong, moved with practiced ease as he set kindling and then logs onto the iron rack. And she couldn't help but remember what it felt like to have those hands moving over her body. When he struck a match to the newspapers balled up beneath the wood, she saw the flickering light play on his features and her heart did that weird little flip-flop she was starting to get used to all over again.

He'd always had that effect on her. From the moment she'd first seen him, Sam Pearce had touched her like no other. There'd been electricity in the air the first time he kissed her, and she'd sworn later that she'd actually seen stars the moment his lips met hers.

But stars and magic and electricity weren't always enough, were they? she mused. Sooner or later, the real world had to intrude on even the most beautiful make-believe worlds. And when it did, it couldn't be ignored.

Sam turned from the fire that crackled and hissed as it gobbled up the fuel in the hearth and just looked at her for a long minute. She tried to read his expression, his eyes, but the light was too dim and maybe she didn't really want to know what he was thinking anyway. Maybe it was best if neither of them gave what was happening here too much thought.

"I've missed you, Michelle," he said quietly.

Oh, no. Her throat tightened up and she had to choke a gulp of air down like a dose of bad-tasting medicine.

"Sam…" She scooted to the edge of the couch and looked around for her purse. Now, her mind screamed. Leave *now*.

Then he held one hand out to her and she had a choice. A very clear choice. She could be smart and get out of that house while the getting was still good…or, she could take his hand and, just for tonight, forget about the lost years. Forget about tomorrow and the inevitable goodbyes to come. Just for tonight, she could hold and be held and pretend that Sam was still hers.

"Michelle?"

She took a breath, then slipped her hand into his.

Five

His fingers curled around hers, and for the first time in ten years, Sam felt...*complete* again. A thought that should have terrified him, because if he'd been thinking clearly he would have realized that his emotions, his *desires,* were dragging him back into a situation he knew would never work. Nothing good could come of this. Nothing permanent. Nothing to build a life on.

There was too much history between them. Too much hurt. Distrust. Betrayal. Hell, *pain.* Whatever it was that sizzled in the air between them at this moment could never be more than just what it was. A stolen moment, snatched from the everyday world.

And, as he looked into her violet eyes, shimmering with the reflected light of the fire, he knew that for right now, it was enough. It was everything. He couldn't let her leave. Not without feeling the magic one more time.

Pulling her off the couch and toward him, he caught her as she fell into his arms. His mouth claimed hers in a frenzy of hot, pulsing need as he eased them both down onto the rug in front of the brick hearth. The snap and crackle of the hungry flames seemed to echo in his bloodstream. He felt scorched from the inside out and still he wanted more. Needed more.

She did, too. He felt it in her response. In the hard embrace of her arms around his neck, in the eager way she pressed her body to his, molding herself against him.

He took her mouth as though he was a one-man invasion force. Parting her lips with his tongue, he pushed into her warmth, stealing her breath and making it his own. Her sighs fed his hunger, his need, and his body hummed with an almost-electrical charge.

He pulled his head back to look at her, and she whispered, "What are we doing, Sam?"

"The only thing we can, Michelle," he told her, then added, "I need to touch you. To feel your skin."

"Oh, yes," she said, and swallowed hard. "I need that, too. So much."

Fingers moving to the buttons on her shirt, Sam had them undone and the material hanging open in seconds. Then he reached inside and cupped one lace-covered breast. His thumb and forefinger circled her nipple again and again, tweaking, teasing, tugging until she writhed beneath him, arching her head back against the rug and moving into his touch, silently demanding more from him. And he gave it to her. Gave it to them both.

He trailed hot, damp kisses down the length of her neck and across her chest until he was stopped by the lacy barrier of her bra. His deft fingers flicked the front closure with an expert snap, and instantly her breasts were open to his gaze. He ran the flat of his hand across the smooth, soft flesh and felt the pebbly surface of her hard nipple against his palm.

Michelle's breath staggered as she arched into him and then she laid her hand atop his, holding him to her, pressing his hand tightly to her body as if afraid he might leave. But Sam had no intention of going anywhere. There was nowhere else in the world he'd rather be at this moment than right here with her. He'd thought about this moment, dreamt about it, fantasized about it for so long, the reality of her presence nearly crushed him.

He threaded his fingers through hers and lifted her hand to one side, holding it down against the floor.

Then he dipped his head and took her nipple into his mouth, letting his tongue swirl around the sensitive tip. She shuddered against him and tightened her grip on his hand. He scraped the edges of his teeth across the hardened bud of flesh until she twisted anxiously in his grasp. Then his lips closed around her, and he suckled her, drawing her essence, her soul deep within himself.

Her hips lifted off the floor as she moved restlessly in tandem with the rhythm of her boiling blood. He felt it. He knew it. Because the same heat was taking him to the edge of control. Again and again, his lips and tongue worked her breasts, each in its turn. He tasted her and with the tasting, tortured them both until even his head spun from the dizzying sensations hurtling through him.

"Sam," she whispered brokenly, and he lifted his head to look into her eyes. "Sam, I need you. I need you inside me. Now. Oh please, now."

"I need it too, baby," he told her, his voice thick with the need strangling him. And suiting action to the words, he released her hand long enough to strip out of his clothes, tossing the T-shirt and jeans over his shoulder into the shadows. Michelle moved just as quickly, peeling her shirt and bra off, then slipping her hands beneath the waistband of her tan slacks.

But when she would have pulled them off, Sam stopped her. Moving to kneel between her legs, he said, "Let me," and she nodded, throat too tight to speak.

His fingers curled beneath the linen fabric and slowly, slowly, he pulled them and her panties down the length of her legs. And every inch of skin he exposed, he kissed, branding her body with the heat of his mouth, with the swipe of his tongue. He felt her body quicken, sensed the urgency building within her. And when he couldn't stand the slow torture a moment longer, he yanked her slacks off and tossed them aside. His gaze swept over her lush body and everything inside him went hot and still.

His hands ached for her. His body throbbed to become a part of her. And still, he wanted more. Wanted to explore every inch of her. To relearn her secrets. To discover this new and yet so achingly familiar Michelle.

She lifted her arms, reaching for him, and he leaned over her, loving the feel of her hands on his skin. He felt the pressure of each one of her fingers as she smoothed her palms up and down his spine, then up and around to his shoulders and chest. When she flicked her thumbnail across his flat nipple, he shuddered and caught her hand tightly.

Twisting his head, he planted a kiss in the center of her palm, then released her and eased back, out of her grasp, out of her reach. Kneeling between her parted thighs, he let his hands explore her damp center. Two fingers slid into her warmth and delved deep. She lifted her hips in response and slapped her hands flat against the floor, as if searching for something to hold onto in her suddenly rocking world.

And while the fingers of his left hand tortured her from the inside, he used his right hand to rub and caress the tiny bud at the core of her. Michelle gasped at his first stroke, feeling the sizzle of white-hot heat pierce her down to her bones. Too much, she thought. Too much sensation at once after so long with nothing. And yet, she wanted more. Wanted his hands on her, his mouth, wanted him to look at her as he was now, with desire burning bright in his eyes.

She watched him watch her. His gaze hooded, his mouth tight, he almost flinched when she groaned his name and rocked her hips against his hand. So long, she thought. So very long since she'd felt anything like this. This magic. This wonder. This amazing connection they shared.

Again and again, his fingers moved in and out of her body, and she felt herself open to him, welcome him. His fingertips worked her sensitive flesh until she quivered in anticipation of the next stroke. The next caress. Her hips rose and fell with the rhythm he set. Her heartbeat pounded and thundered in her chest until all she heard was the roaring of her own blood in her ears and the hissing crackle of the fire.

Backlit by the flickering flames, Sam took his hands from her. Before she could protest their loss, he scooped her behind off the floor and lifted her body until her legs hung helplessly on either side of him.

Oh my, she thought wildly, clutching at the rug beneath her. She knew what was coming next and heaven help her, she wanted it so desperately, she could hardly breathe with the need choking her.

And then Sam bent his head and took her with his mouth. His lips closed over her most delicate flesh and his tongue explored her damp heat with long, quick strokes that fed the flames licking at her soul.

She twisted in his grasp, her head moving from side to side, her gaze locked on him, watching him take her. "Sam," she managed to say on a half moan. "Oh, Sam, don't stop."

He lifted his head long enough to meet her gaze and promise, "Not a chance." Then his fingers curled into the soft flesh of her behind, gripping her tightly as he bent to reclaim her. His lips, his tongue, his teeth drove her into a frenzy that quickened her heart even as it shallowed her breath. Michelle felt her climax coming. From somewhere deep within her body, she felt the tightening, the growing, pulsing ache and she fought against the onslaught. She wanted to make this last forever. She wanted this one moment to stretch into eternity.

But Sam was determined. And he wasn't a man to be denied.

His tongue swirled over and around the bud of her

sex while he slipped two fingers into her depths again and this time, Michelle couldn't hold it off. The first wave hit her so hard that she called his name in a choked-off cry and slapped her hands hard against the floor once more. Her hips bucked in his grasp. She forced herself to keep her eyes open and locked on him as the second wave carried her over the edge of need into the well of completion.

And before her body had stopped quivering, he set her down and pushed himself home. She looked up into his eyes. He braced his hands on either side of her head and delved deeper, thrusting himself so far into her body that she was sure she felt him touch her heart.

Her legs locked around his middle, pinning him to her, holding him captive inside her while she gloried in the strong, hard feel of him atop her, within her, again. So familiar, she thought. So...*right.*

"I need you," he whispered, locking his gaze with hers. "Damn it, I still need you."

A sting of tears burned her eyes at the desperate tone of his voice, but a moment later, all else was forgotten as he moved against her. He led her in the dance. A frantic, pulsing rhythm pushed them both, demanding to be fed. To be recognized. And with every thrust of his body, Sam laid siege to her heart and soul.

She clung to his shoulders, tightened her legs around his hips and moved with him, silently giving him all he'd given her. Showing him the only way she could that she too, still needed.

A swirl of sensation coiled within her and Michelle felt the tension in her body mount again. She moved into him, matching him stroke for stroke, kissing him, touching him, chasing that wild, indescribable feeling. Wanting it again. Wanting to share it with him. Be one with him when the magic took him.

And when at last it came in a crashing blow, it took them both. He shouted her name, and she didn't know whether he meant it as a curse or a blessing. But then she was tumbling over a precipice, and Sam cradled her in his arms to soften her fall.

Three hours later, Michelle groaned and eased into a sitting position. Staring into the embers of the dying fire, she said softly, "Okay, that was probably a mistake."

Sam stirred beside her, then went up on one elbow. "Which time?" he asked.

She looked at him over her shoulder and tried to fight down the instant flash of desire that splintered in her bloodstream and sent sparks shooting along her veins. Good heavens. They'd already done the deed three times now. When would enough be enough?

He lifted one hand and rubbed the back of his neck and she watched the play of muscles across his chest.

Her mouth went dry. Oh, perfect. Apparently, she'd never be able to get enough of him.

Which was just one more reason why this should never have happened. "Maybe we should check on the girls again."

"We just did. You're stalling. Which time was a mistake?"

"Any of them," she said. "Heck, *all* of them."

"You didn't seem to mind at the time," he pointed out.

True, she thought. Too true. Not only had she not minded, she'd darn near raped him the last time. The poor man had been exhausted, and she'd simply climbed atop him, assuring him that she'd do all the work.

She moaned softly and dropped her head into her cupped palms. It had been so long since they'd been together, and tonight it had felt like just yesterday. Her mind whirled drunkenly from one thought to the next. She sighed when she remembered how long it had taken for her to recover from the loss of him the last time. And now she'd set herself up for more pain. For heaven's sake, what had she been thinking? The answer was simple, of course. She hadn't been thinking at all. She'd been feeling. And, oh boy, what a feeling!

Michelle lifted her head and looked into the fire. Blackened bits of wood clung to the iron grate, and here and there red glowed like the eyes of the damned. *Great analogy,* she thought. *Feeling a little guilty, are we?*

She hadn't meant for this to happen, she assured herself. She'd only been trying to be neighborly. Friendly. Helpful.

And then she'd helped herself to his body. Again and again.

Oh, good grief.

"I have to go," she said abruptly, and swung her head from side to side, searching for her clothes.

"Well," he said slowly. "That didn't take long."

Michelle stopped dead and looked at him. "What's that supposed to mean?"

"Just what you think it does," he said, and sat up beside her. His arm brushed against hers and a rush of heat pooled at her center.

She ignored it. "Why don't you tell me?"

"Fine. You're running away again."

Her jaw dropped, closed, then dropped again. "I am *not* running away. I'm just leaving...quickly. And what the heck do you mean, 'again?'"

"You practically chased me off with a stick, remember? You were running then and you're running now."

"That wasn't running," she snapped defensively as she turned her head, searching for her clothes. "We broke up."

"*You* broke us up."

"I had my reasons," she said. Where in the heck did her clothes get to?

"Which you never bothered to share with me," he reminded her.

A small stab of guilt poked at her, but she buried it quickly. She wouldn't feel badly about doing what had had to be done. "The reasons weren't important," she said.

"Maybe not to you," he countered, grabbing her arm and turning her so that she was forced to look at him. "But when somebody rips my heart out and then stomps on it, I get a little curious as to why."

She was cold now and getting colder. Strange that, when she'd been so heated just moments ago. But then the fire in his eyes had kept her warm, and now she saw only frost in those green depths.

"So tell me," he said, his fingers tightening on her upper arm.

She glanced down at his hand, then up into his eyes again. "You're hurting me."

He released her instantly and shook his head. "Sorry. Didn't mean to." Then he leaned to one side, snagged her bra off a brass lamp and handed it to her. "But I still want an answer to my question. Why'd you do it? Why'd you leave me?"

Slipping into her bra, she hooked the darn thing and suddenly felt more naked than she had all night. She didn't want to talk about the past. It wouldn't do either of them any good and besides, she wasn't about to tell him her reasons. They were her own.

"I don't want to talk about it, Sam," she said, and spotted her blouse, crumpled on the floor, half under a chair. She reached for it and tugged it on. Now all she needed was her pants, and she could get the heck out of here.

"Well, why didn't you say so?" he countered, sarcasm coloring his tone darkly. "Hey, if Michelle doesn't want to talk about something, it doesn't get talked about, right?"

"There's no reason to be snotty."

"Excuse the hell outa me," he snapped. "But the etiquette of having incredible sex with an ex-girlfriend is something I've never been real clear on."

She muttered something, and he said, "What was that?"

"I *said*," she repeated, "you might try going with the old standards. *If you can't say something nice, don't say anything at all.*"

"You're really something, you know that?" he asked, and stood up. Grabbing his jeans off the couch, he pulled them on and zipped them closed. "You crash back into my life, twist it all around and then want to crash back out again."

"Sam—"

"Who are you anyway? Old Faithful? Every ten years you stop by to screw with my head?"

"That's not fair," she said.

"Maybe not, but it's accurate."

Her gaze flicked around the room again. At last! She grabbed her underwear, then saw her slacks and scuttled toward them. Once she'd pulled them on, she faced him with a bit more confidence than she'd had naked. Pushing her hair back from her face, she said, "I didn't mean for this to happen, you know."

A long moment passed before he sighed heavily, folded his arms across his chest and admitted, "Yeah. Neither did I."

"Then maybe we ought to just chalk it up to 'old times' and let it go."

"Can you?" he asked, and even from halfway across the room his gaze seemed to burrow deep inside her, probing, seeking for a truth he wanted to hear but was afraid he wouldn't.

"I have to," she said simply, then grabbed up her purse and headed for the front door while she still could.

She had the door open when his voice stopped her.

"Michelle."

She glanced at him over her shoulder. "Yes?"

"Thanks for helping. With the babies, I mean."

"Anytime," she managed to say before her throat closed with emotion. Then she left the pretty little house and the man she'd always loved, closing the door quietly behind her.

Six

For a week and a half, Sam tried everything to keep his new world spinning on its axis. But no matter what he did, the damn thing kept careening off into space.

He'd gone through two nannies, about five-thousand diapers, a full bottle of aspirin and only God knew how many loads of laundry. And he'd come to one conclusion.

As a father, he made a great Marine.

And now his most recent attempt at normalcy was walking out the door.

"Those babies need discipline, Gunnery Sergeant," the nanny said, pausing to adjust her tiny black hat atop her tidy gray curls. "Without discipline, there is chaos."

One dark eyebrow lifted, and Sam said, "Chaos? They can't even talk yet."

She sniffed and pursed her lips, and Sam had a flashback to his fourth-grade teacher, Mrs. Henry. The woman had had the soul of a prune and the disposition of a rattler. He had the distinct impression this woman and his former teacher had a lot in common.

Hadn't he walked into the house just a while ago to hear both babies wailing while their "nanny" sat uncaring, reading a book? When he'd asked her why she wasn't attending to the children, the old bat had told him flatly that to pick up a crying child only taught it to cry whenever it wanted something.

Of course, since babies had no other way of communicating, Sam had always figured that's what they were *supposed* to do.

"One must have rules," the woman said, bringing him back to the here and now. "As a military man, surely you can appreciate that." Then, without waiting for an answer, she spun around and left.

Silently, Sam told himself she'd have made a better general than a nanny. Anyone who actually expected nine-month-old children to follow rules had no business pretending to be a caregiver.

Yet, even knowing he—and the babies—were better off without her, watching the woman walk down the drive toward the street filled Sam with a desperation he hadn't known in years. He had to find *someone* to love and care for these kids while he was at work.

Miranda Fortune, his aunt, he reminded himself, had recommended the nanny service. And though he knew she'd only been trying to help, it hadn't worked out real well. The first nanny had been little more than a kid herself, and this last one…well, she was gone now, too. Which left him up the proverbial creek without so much as a boat, let alone a paddle.

And he wasn't about to call Miranda and tell her it hadn't worked out. She'd only try to help again, and frankly, Sam didn't want to feel even more indebted to the family he'd only recently acquired. He scrubbed one hand across his face. The fact that he'd called on his new family at all was a measure of just how desperate he'd become. Sam wasn't a man to go running for help. He usually preferred to solve his own problems. To straighten out his own messes.

But damned if he could handle this problem alone. He backed into the house and closed the front door. Walking down the hall, he stopped in the open doorway to the girls' room and leaned one shoulder against the jamb.

Sleeping, both of them. They'd exhausted themselves in a futile quest for attention. The Crier… *Beth,* he told himself sternly, was curled up into a ball, sucking on her thumb. Silvery tracks of tears shed still lay on her round cheeks and Sam winced before shifting his gaze to the other baby that was now his responsibility. Marie lay sprawled in her bed, her right arm tucked around a stuffed lamb she'd already become attached to.

These two children were counting on him. Depending on him to create a home, a safe place for them. And he didn't even know how to start. Shoving one hand across the top of his head, he tried to figure out how a man who knew next to nothing of families could be expected to give these girls what they needed.

Then Beth sniffled in her sleep, and the soft sound jabbed at him, prodding him to do the one thing he'd told himself he wouldn't.

He turned around to look at the phone sitting on a table in the living room. "You've got two choices here," he muttered to himself. "You can keep on stumbling around blindly, or you can swallow your pride and call Michelle."

Hell, it had taken all of his self-control to keep from doing just that for the last ten days. He'd promised himself not to go back down that road again. But he missed her, damn it.

He'd tried not to. And God knew he'd been busy enough that he shouldn't have had time to think about her. But somehow, she was always there, at the edges of his mind, haunting him with memories of their last night together, with images of what might have been.

Calling her now would only open the door to more trouble. More complications. He walked across the room, picked up the phone and stared at the keypad. And even as his fingers punched out her number, he told himself he was making a mistake.

Then she answered the phone and nothing else mattered but the sound of her voice.

Michelle had buried herself in her work for a week and a half. Her event-planning business had finally taken off, and she had two birthday parties, a wedding and a baby shower to arrange. She didn't have time to worry about Sam and those babies.

At least, that's what she had told herself every time her brain had strayed from the project at hand to the little house on the other side of town. But she couldn't seem to help herself. She wondered if the babies were settling in. She wondered if Sam had found someone reliable to take care of them while he was at work. And she wondered if he missed her half as much as she did him.

Disgusted, she turned off her laptop computer and gently closed the lid. How was she supposed to concentrate on Jonathon Murray's fortieth birthday party when Sam's face kept appearing in her mind? Standing up, she walked around the edge of her kitchen table and stared out the window. She hardly noticed the sunshine filtering through the oaks to lay in a speckled pattern on the grass three floors below. She paid no attention to the usual bustle of the busy street.

Her gaze softened, focus blurred and instead of the world outside her apartment, she saw Sam's face. She could almost taste his kiss. Feel his hands on her body. Everything inside her tightened.

And then the phone rang, splintering the image, and she wasn't sure if she was grateful or disappointed.

"For heaven's sake," she muttered, shaking her head as she moved to the phone. This daydreaming about Sam had to stop. Snatching it up before it could ring again, she answered, "Hello?"

"Michelle?"

Sam's voice. Her fingers tightened on the receiver and a ripple of anticipation rolled along her spine. She tried to ignore it, but then realized it was pointless. This was simply how she reacted to Sam, so instead of trying to disregard the effect he had on her, maybe it'd be better if she simply found a way to live with it.

Sure, she thought. Shouldn't be too tough. Sort of like learning to live with being on fire. Okay, she told herself, be calm. Be cool. Be casual. She could do this. If she could convince her heart to leave her throat.

"Hi Sam," she said, and twirled her fingers

around the telephone cord tightly. "Didn't expect to hear from you." Oh, good, she told herself, rubbing the spot between her eyebrows. That was casual. Attack.

"Didn't think you'd want me to call," he countered, "after you cut and ran the other night..."

"Cut and ran?" she repeated, lifting her head and glaring at the wall. "I didn't run, I left."

"Yeah," he said, "I remember you leaving—the other night *and* ten years ago."

"I had my reasons for leaving ten years ago."

"Too bad you never bothered to share 'em."

She would not be drawn back into this old argument. She would not be put in the position of having to defend her decision. Wasn't it enough that she'd paid the price of losing him?

"Look Sam," she said, fingers squeezing the cord tightly enough to break the connection, "I don't have to explain myself to you."

"So you've said."

"Will you let it go already?"

He sighed into the phone, and she heard the weariness in his tone when he spoke again. "This isn't why I called."

"Why did you then?" she asked stiffly. "If you weren't looking to pick a fight, I mean?"

He paused, she heard him take a deep breath and blow it out again, and she waited.

"Actually," he said slowly, "it's about the twins."

"What is it?" she asked, anger forgotten in a rush of concern, "are they all right?"

"Yeah, they're fine. It's just that…" Another pause, and then a stream of words left him in a rush, tumbling over each other. Almost as if he wanted to say what he had to say before he changed his mind. "Look, Michelle, I'm in a bind, and I could really use your help. I know I'm in no position to ask it, especially after starting off this phone call the way I did, but I'm asking anyway."

She blinked, pulled the receiver away from her ear and stared at it for a second or two. Sam Pearce admitting he needed *help?* And coming to *her?* Boy, he must really be desperate, she thought.

"I need somebody who can watch the girls—temporarily I mean, until I can find someone permanent."

"But you have a nanny service, don't you?" she asked, and as soon as the words left her mouth, she winced and slapped her forehead with the palm of one hand.

"How did you know that?"

Well, good. Now he knew that she'd been keeping tabs on him and the babies. What next? she asked herself. Going to confess to driving down his street three or four times this week in the hopes of catching a glimpse of either him or the girls? Nope, she thought quickly. That little secret stays a secret.

But to answer his question, she muttered, "Miranda told me." She didn't tell him that she'd badgered her friend for information and had sworn her to secrecy, as well.

"You know Miranda," he said, and it wasn't a question.

"Uh-huh." Michelle spoke up again quickly, diverting the conversation. "So what happened to the nanny?"

"They didn't work out."

"They?" He'd had more than one nanny in less than two weeks?

"It's a long story," he said, then added, "but the upshot of it is, I still need someone to help me with these babies for a while."

"Why me?" she asked, even though everything inside her was telling her to say yes.

"Because no matter what's between us, I trust you with them. They responded to you that first night." He took a breath and said, "I need you, Michelle. I need help."

A flutter around her heart made Michelle reach out, grab a kitchen chair and pull it toward her. He needed her. There was trouble here, she told herself. Possible complications. Possible heartbreak. And she wanted to say yes anyway. Her arms ached to hold those babies.

And yet…being in the same house as Sam, on a daily basis…she plopped down onto the chair, sucked in a deep breath to steady her heartbeat and forced herself to say, "Oh, Sam, I don't know if that's a good idea."

"I know what you're thinking."

"Oh, I doubt that," she said as an image of Sam, bending over her, his naked body covering hers, floated through her mind. Darn it. She couldn't go back there again. She couldn't allow herself to be swept up into a passionate fling that would only end in pain.

Firmly, she pushed those images out of her mind and told herself silently to cut it out. "There would have to be some ground rules."

"What kind of ground rules?" he asked, suspicion coloring his tone.

"The kind that will keep what happened the other night from happening again."

"Like?"

"Like," she said, "no touching. There will be no touching of any kind between us."

"Okay."

"And no kissing," she said quickly, even as she remembered the taste of his lips on hers.

"That pretty much falls into the touching area, doesn't it?"

"Just making sure," she said.

"Fine. No touching. No kissing. Then we have a deal?"

Oh, she would probably regret this. But if she didn't do it, she would regret that, too. So, if she was going to be miserable anyway, she might as well do what she so desperately wanted to do.

"Deal," she said before any stray rational thought could object. "I'll be there in the morning."

At seven the next morning, Sam opened his door to Michelle and took just a moment to enjoy the sight of her. Damned if she didn't look good even in jeans and a sweatshirt. Her hair was swept up into a ponytail, and she'd tied a lavender scarf around it. The silky fabric flew about her face in the soft wind and the color of the scarf seemed to intensify the violet of her eyes.

Raising an eyebrow, she asked, "Do I get to come inside?"

"Oh," he said, startled out of his thoughts. "Yeah, sure." He stepped back, and she walked past him, her shoulder brushing against his chest, setting off lightning-bolt-like spears of heat that rocketed through him right down to the soles of his feet. *No touching,* he remembered and silently told himself it was a good rule—but one that was going to be very difficult to abide by. He inhaled sharply, and the faint fragrance of her perfume enveloped him in a hazy mist of lavender and vanilla. Sam swallowed hard and asked himself for the hundredth time if he was doing the right thing here.

But, even as the question rose in his mind, he knew he hadn't had a choice. He needed help, and, despite their past history, he trusted Michelle to take good care of those kids. She might break his heart every ten years or so, but the twins would be safe with her.

Closing the door, he turned to look at her as she set her purse and a nylon computer case down onto the sofa. Apparently, she planned on getting some work done today, too. Then she shoved her hands into the back pockets of her jeans and rocked back and forth on her heels.

"So," she said, glancing at the hallway leading to the bedrooms, "are they awake?"

He snorted a laugh. "Only since five."

She nodded and shifted her gaze to his. "Is this going to work, Sam?"

He knew what she was talking about and it had nothing to do with her abilities to care for the twins. "I don't know," he said, figuring honesty was the only way to go here. Besides, she'd have known he was lying if he'd said anything else.

Not much point in trying to deny the fire to the very person who was standing beside you in the flames.

His gaze slid over her quickly and then came to

rest on the words emblazoned across the front of her sweatshirt. " 'Events with Flair'?" he asked.

She pulled her hands out of her pockets and ran one palm across the front of her shirt. "It's my company. My business." Then, as if grasping at a safe topic, she went on, "I plan events. Weddings, parties, conferences."

"Any good at it?" he asked.

"Darn good."

He didn't doubt it. In fact, he was pretty sure there wasn't a thing Michelle couldn't do if she put her mind to it. That is, except marry him when he asked. Okay, best not go down that road right now.

Changing the subject, he led the way down the hall toward the girls' room, talking to Michelle as he went. "I fed 'em both an hour ago, but they insisted on wearing more of the food than they ate, so they'll probably be hungry again soon."

"Okay," she said. She was just a step behind him. He hadn't needed to hear her voice to know that, of course. He could sense her closeness. Feel the heat from her body.

He stepped into what was now the nursery and laughed shortly at the surprised expressions on the two tiny faces looking at him. Beth was standing up in her crib, small fists wrapped tightly around the rail as she bounced up and down on her mattress. Marie sat in the middle of her bed, with the lamb on her lap as she babbled incoherently.

But when they saw him, their eyes widened and twin smiles creased round, dimpled faces. Sam's heart twisted in his chest as if it was being wrung out by four tiny hands. They'd gotten to him. And damned if they didn't know it. It was hard to believe that two weeks ago they'd been little more to him than photos sent from proud parents. Now, he could hardly imagine his house without the sounds of baby laugher and the scent of milk and powder.

Marie pulled herself up in the crib, and instantly her diaper fell off. Sam scowled. He was still having trouble with those things.

"Honestly, Sam," Michelle said as she walked past him toward the now-naked baby, "you don't know how to make a diaper stay on?"

"I think she pulls it off," he said in his own defense. Sending a quick look at the other baby, he noted, "Beth's diaper is still on."

Michelle looked, too. "Barely, and you've got the tape stuck to her belly."

He looked closer and frowned. "They move around a lot. It's not easy, you know."

Shaking her head, Michelle laid Marie down on her bed and said, "Hand me a fresh diaper, will you?"

Sam snatched one up from the ever-present stack near the foot of the crib and handed it over. Then, leaning his forearms on the foot rail, he watched as Marie bicycled her little legs as if she were in an

Ironman triathlon. Smiling to himself he said, "Okay, Michelle. Let's see *you* get around those flailing legs."

She turned her head and looked at him. One eyebrow lifted as she asked, "Is that a challenge?"

"Oh, it's a challenge, all right."

"You're on," she said, and turned back to the baby. Picking up the stuffed lamb, she held it close to Marie, nuzzling the soft animal's nose against hers. The baby laughed, made a grab for the toy and held it tight. And while she was distracted, Michelle opened a diaper, slid it into place and quickly taped it closed.

"Ta-da," she said, lifting both hands in the air like a rodeo queen who'd just roped a calf.

"You cheated," Sam said, straightening up from the crib and giving his new daughter a look that plainly said, *traitor*.

"I didn't cheat," Michelle argued. "Wasn't it you who once told me that a Marine had to Improvise, Overcome and Adapt?"

"That's Improvise, Adapt and Overcome," he corrected.

"I just said that."

"Not in the right order."

"What difference does that make?"

"One's right," he said, "one's wrong."

She shook her head. "Okay." Inhaling sharply,

she said, "Anyway, in whatever order, that's what I did."

And the pleased grin on her face was electrifying. He had to force himself not to move closer. Not to reach out and cup her cheek, smooth the pad of his thumb across her skin. Not to pull her close and claim her mouth in a kiss he'd been hungering for since their last night together.

Which reminded him of something else they had to discuss before they could enter into their new bargain. He'd been putting it off for more than a week, knowing that if he came within a foot of her, a discussion wouldn't be paramount in his mind. But he couldn't delay this little talk any longer.

"Michelle," he said quietly, and her smile slowly faded at the seriousness of his tone. "We have to talk about the other night."

Her features closed up. He could have sworn he actually saw a shutter drop over her eyes. But this had to be said, whether she wanted to talk about it or not.

"There's nothing to talk about," she said. "We both agreed it was a mistake. It's over. Let it go."

"We can't. Not yet, anyway."

"Sam, our deal was—"

"The deal was, no more touching," he interrupted. "But there was already a lot of touching between us."

"Sam, there's no point in talking about this," she told him. "It'll only make things harder."

They couldn't get much harder, he thought. Here he stood, beside the woman who'd haunted his dreams for years, and he was just as far away from her now as he ever was. What could be harder than that?

"Damn it, Michelle," he said, his voice tightening in response to the frustration clawing at him. "We have to talk about something we *should* have talked about that night." Catching her gaze with his, he looked deep into the eyes staring at him and said, "We didn't take any precautions, remember? I need to know if you were protected."

Seven

Anger bubbled inside Sam. The Queen of Denial, he thought, watching her gaze shift from the baby to the wall. She'd once again denied what was between them without even giving him an explanation. Well, this time she was damn well going to talk to him. He needed to know if there was a chance he'd soon be a father of *three*.

"Michelle?"

She inhaled sharply, glanced at him and said, "It's a little late to be worrying about that."

And he knew it. Worrying about pregnancies wasn't just *her* responsibility. But damn it, touching her after ten long years had been like being electrocuted. He'd been lucky he remembered to breathe. "Yeah, I know," he said, angry at himself for letting this happen. But it *had* happened, and they *would* deal with it. Better late than never. "I wasn't thinking then. *We* weren't thinking that night."

She almost flinched, and he wondered if she was remembering, as he was, the feel of him sliding into her body. The thundering of their heartbeats. The swell of sensation. Good grief, just remembering it had him hard and ready all over again.

"I know," she said, and finally looked him square in the eye. "But that was a mistake. It won't happen again."

Strange how empty a man could feel on hearing those words from the woman he wanted so badly. Still, it was better this way, he told himself. No point in going down a road that he already knew came to a dead end.

"Yeah," he said tightly, "we already established that. But you haven't answered the question, either. And just so you know, if you're willing to take my word for it, I can tell you that I'm healthy. You don't have to worry on that score."

What an idiot she was. Michelle hadn't even considered *that*. And in this day and age, that was ridiculous. But she did trust him not to lie to her. So she said, "Thank you. I do believe you. And you should know that I'm...fine, too."

She knew she was healthy. There had only been two men in her life. Sam and her late husband. And since William had died, she'd pretty much been living a nunlike life.

A reluctant smile curved his lips. "I didn't figure you were anything else, Michelle. But there's still the chance of a pregnancy. Unless..."

A knot formed in her stomach and crowded up her throat. "You don't have to worry about that."

"You're sure there's no chance?"

Everything in her went cold and still. A small, nearly forgotten ache settled around the base of her heart as she said, "Positive."

"Oh." He nodded abruptly. "Well, that's good then, isn't it?"

"Yes, it is," she said, turning from him to smile down at Marie. The baby cooed at her and blew a spit bubble. Oh, yeah, she thought. It was a real good thing that she didn't have to worry about becoming pregnant. What a lucky break.

She reached down and stroked Marie's cheek, luxuriating in the downy softness of the baby's skin. How fortunate for her that she'd never have to be concerned about being a mother. That she'd never know what it was like to feel a child growing inside her. Or to hold a brand-new life in her arms and know that somehow she'd produced a miracle.

A sheen of tears filmed her vision and she blinked them back, refusing to let them fall, refusing to let

Sam see her cry. He'd only want to know why, and she couldn't tell him the reason now, any more than she could have ten years ago. Besides, she told herself firmly as she took hold of the emotion sweeping through her, she'd cried her tears a long time ago. She'd learned to live with the fact that she would never be able to have a baby.

And revisiting that pain...that emptiness...was something she simply couldn't bear to do.

"Hey," he said softly, reaching out to lay one hand on her forearm. "Are you okay?"

No sympathy, she thought. It would be her undoing. And no touching. The feel of his hand on her sent prisms of heat shattering throughout her body. Everything in her wanted to move into him, hold him, be held by him. She wanted that rush of sensation one more time before sentencing herself to a lifetime without him. But she couldn't. Not now. Not ever. Nothing had changed. The situation was as it had been ten years ago. He was a man who wanted, *needed* family. And she was a woman who couldn't give him that.

Sniffing slightly, she straightened her spine, lifted her chin and deliberately stepped out of his reach. "I'm fine," she said, and put every ounce of conviction she could spare into the lie.

Then reaching down, she lifted Marie out of her crib and as the baby wrapped pudgy arms around her neck, Michelle held the child like a barrier between her and Sam. "Aren't you late for work?" she asked briskly, watching him, hoping the wary suspicion would disappear from his eyes.

The distraction worked.

He checked his wristwatch, muttered, "Damn it, yes, I am," then headed for the door. He paused at the threshold and looked back at her. "You're sure you're all right with this?"

"For heaven's sake, Sam," she said. "They're babies, not nuclear reactors. I can handle this."

He nodded. "Right. Okay then. See you guys later."

Then he was gone. The front door slammed behind him and a moment or two later, she heard his car's engine roar into life. Michelle looked out the window and watched as he backed into the tree-lined street and drove away. As his car disappeared from view, she took her first easy breath since entering the house.

Marie gurgled and smacked her little hands against Michelle's face, and she gave the baby a smile. No matter what else happened, she was going to enjoy this time with the babies. And if she pretended, just for a little while, that the twins were *her* children, what harm could it do? Soon enough this temporary situation would end, and Sam wouldn't need her help any more and she'd return to her regular life. In her too-clean, too-quiet apartment, she'd have all the time in the world to mourn the loss of Sam and these

PLAY BANGO!

AND GET THREE FREE GIFTS!

It looks like BINGO, it plays like BINGO but it's FREE!

HOW TO PLAY:

1. With a coin, scratch the Caller Card to reveal your 5 lucky numbers and see that they match your Bango Card. Then check the claim chart to discover what we have for you — 2 FREE BOOKS and a FREE GIFT — ALL YOURS, ALL FREE!

2. Send back the Bango card and you'll receive two brand-new Silhouette Desire® novels. These books have a cover price of $3.99 each in the U.S. and $4.50 each in Canada, but they are yours to keep absolutely free.

3. There's no catch. You're under no obligation to buy anything. We charge nothing — ZERO — for your first shipment. And you don't have to make any minimum number of purchases — not even one!

4. The fact is, thousands of readers enjoy receiving our books by mail from the Silhouette Reader Service™. They enjoy the convenience of home delivery…they like getting the best new novels at discount prices, BEFORE they're available in stores…and they love their *Heart to Heart* subscriber newsletter featuring author news, horoscopes, recipes, book reviews and much more!

5. We hope that after receiving your free books you'll want to remain a subscriber. But the choice is yours — to continue or cancel, any time at all! So why not take us up on our invitation, with no risk of any kind. You'll be glad you did!

YOURS FREE!

This exciting mystery gift is yours free when you play BANGO!

Visit us online at
www.eHarlequin.com

It's fun, and we're giving away
FREE GIFTS
to all players!

PLAY BANGO!

SCRATCH HERE! →

CALLER CARD

YES!

Please send me the 2 free books and the gift for which I qualify! I understand that I am under no obligation to purchase any books as explained on the back of this card.

YOUR CARD ↓

BANGO				
38	9	44	10	38
92	7	5	27	14
2	51	FREE	91	67
75	3	12	20	13
6	15	26	50	31

CLAIM CHART!

Match 5 numbers	2 FREE BOOKS & A MYSTERY GIFT
Match 4 numbers	2 FREE BOOKS
Match 3 numbers	1 FREE BOOK

(S-D-OS-12/01)

326 SDL DHZ3   **225 SDL DHZ2**

NAME   (PLEASE PRINT CLEARLY)

ADDRESS

APT.#   CITY

STATE/PROV.   ZIP/POSTAL CODE

Offer limited to one per household and not valid to current Silhouette Desire® subscribers.
All orders subject to approval.

The Silhouette Reader Service™ — Here's how it works:

Accepting your 2 free books and gift places you under no obligation to buy anything. You may keep the books and gift and return the shipping statement marked "cancel." If you do not cancel, about a month later we'll send you 6 additional novels and bill you just $3.34 each in the U.S., or $3.74 each in Canada, plus 25¢ shipping & handling per book and applicable taxes if any.* That's the complete price and — compared to cover prices of $3.99 each in the U.S. and $4.50 each in Canada — it's quite a bargain! You may cancel at any time, but if you choose to continue, every month we'll send you 6 more books, which you may either purchase at the discount price or return to us and cancel your subscription.

*Terms and prices subject to change without notice. Sales tax applicable in N.Y. Canadian residents will be charged applicable provincial taxes and GST.

If offer card is missing write to: Silhouette Reader Service, 3010 Walden Ave., P.O. Box 1867, Buffalo, NY 14240-1867

NO POSTAGE
NECESSARY
IF MAILED
IN THE
UNITED STATES

BUSINESS REPLY MAIL
FIRST-CLASS MAIL   PERMIT NO. 717-003   BUFFALO, NY

POSTAGE WILL BE PAID BY ADDRESSEE

SILHOUETTE READER SERVICE
3010 WALDEN AVE
PO BOX 1867
BUFFALO NY 14240-9952

children. Wouldn't it be better if she had a few memories to make the emptiness waiting ahead a little less...*empty?*

She dropped a soft kiss on the top of Marie's head and inhaled the scent that was powdery and sweet and pure baby. And an ache she knew she would always carry settled in a tiny corner of her heart.

Sam took the signed papers from the kid sitting opposite him and looked them over one more time, making sure every *i* was dotted and every *t* crossed. When he'd satisfied himself, he held out his right hand toward the new recruit.

"Looks like you're set, Mr. Jackson," he said. "You'll report for boot camp in six weeks. You'll be notified as to time and place."

As the kid shook his hand and then stood up smiling, Sam idly tried to recall a time when he'd been that young. That eager to start a career in the Marines.

"Thank you, sir," Henry Jackson, freshly signed Marine boot said.

Sam shook his head and stood up. "Gunnery Sergeant, Mr. Jackson. You don't call Sergeants, 'sir'. We're not officers. We *work* for a living."

"Yes, sir, Gunnery Sergeant." Then, still grinning, he turned around and marched at full attention out the door of the recruitment station and into the sunshine.

Someone behind Sam chuckled and he half turned to smile at Staff Sergeant Jake Cutter. "Is it me," Sam asked, "or are these kids getting younger every year?"

"It's not you, Sam," Jake told him with a slow shake of his head. "They *are* younger. Hell, the only other alternative is that *we're* getting old, and I don't accept that."

"Me, neither," Sam said and sat down to file Henry Jackson's recruitment papers.

"So," Jake asked, swiveling in his seat until the ancient wooden desk chair creaked like an old man getting out of a tub, "how's life in Romper Room?"

"Crazed," Sam answered simply. Jake had been hearing about every complaint and every victory since the moment Marie and Beth had entered his life. God, was it only a couple of weeks ago? The whole damn world had changed in just a couple of weeks?

He leaned back in his own chair, staring out the storefront window at the scene beyond. All right, he told himself. Maybe it wasn't the *entire* world that had changed. The view out the window was the same as always. Pedestrians hustled from one store to the next, intent on their business while skateboarding teenagers made the whole place an obstacle course.

He'd been in the recruitment office two months and still had nearly a year to go on this duty assignment. Damn shame, he thought, since working recruitment gave a man too much time to think. What he needed was action. Something to do. Troops to prepare for combat. Enemies to attack. Something to focus himself on. Something to take his mind off Michelle and the twins and the rest of his life.

Sighing, he clapped one hand over his eyes. He was just tired, he assured himself. That's why thoughts of Michelle plagued him. That's why he couldn't seem to keep his mind from veering toward her. Fatigue could really mess a man up. Hell, he hadn't had a decent night's sleep since the twins arrived. And he couldn't really blame it on them, either.

They weren't crying all night, it was just that Sam seemed to hear every breath they took—every sniffle and sigh and he found himself getting up five times a night just to make sure they were still breathing. And for a man who used to brag about being able to sleep through a mortar attack, that was saying something.

"Why the hell are you doing this, Sam?"

Pathetically grateful for the distraction, he left his turbulent thoughts behind and turned to look at his friend. "Doing what?"

Jake leaned forward in his chair, propped his forearms on his thighs and studied him. "Keeping those girls. You don't have to," he said.

Sam's features tightened, but Jake kept talking.

"Hell, you could sign over custody to the state."

''Can't do that,'' he muttered, though it shamed him to admit he'd actually considered that option for about ten full minutes when he'd first heard about Dave and Jackie's accident. But what single man wouldn't have thought about trying to get out of the responsibility of becoming an overnight father? That was then, though. The decision was made now. The situation was set. The girls were his, and they would stay his. It was the way Dave had wanted it. And the promise Sam had made to his dead friend would be kept.

''Nobody should expect you to turn your life upside down,'' Jake told him.

The babies had a right to expect that, Sam thought. They'd lost everything—and it was up to him to try to make it up to them. He briefly rubbed his eyes with his fingertips and shifted his shoulders as if trying to ease the weighty burden that was settled on his back. Not that the babies themselves were the burden. It was the responsibility of trying to give them the life they should have had that worried Sam.

Hell, what he didn't know about families could fill at least a couple of encyclopedia volumes. No pressure, he told himself wryly.

All he said to Jake though, was, ''Dave would expect it. I made the man a promise, and he'd damn well expect me to keep it.''

''Dave's dead,'' Jake said quietly. ''I mean it's a

shame, but there it is. The man's dead and he wouldn't know if you kept that promise or not.''

Sam's jaw got tight. "*I'd* know."

"Man, you've got a thick skull," Jake said, disgusted. "There's couples all over the place just dying to adopt babies, Sam. Those twins would find a good home in a heartbeat."

"They've got a good home," Sam said stubbornly. At least, they would have, as soon as he got everything sorted out and running in an efficient, military manner.

"Fine. But most single fathers aren't Marines, who are going to have to worry about deploying."

Sam turned and looked at him.

Jake nodded as comprehension slowly dawned on Sam's face. "Now you're getting it," he said. "Hadn't thought about that, had you?"

No, he hadn't. Sam rubbed one hand across the back of his neck as his mind raced. Every Marine had to be able to be deployed. Which meant a parent *had* to have a guardian—a caretaker—for his or her child. Someone with whom the kid could stay while the deployed Marine was gone for up to six months at a stretch.

And if you couldn't deploy…you couldn't be a Marine.

"Damn it."

"I knew you'd get it," Jake said wryly. "Eventually."

Okay fine. It was a snag in the plan. A small problem. Well, maybe a *huge* problem. But it could be solved. All it would take is a little thought. A little imagination.

After all, it wasn't like he was completely alone, anymore. He had family now. Granted, it wasn't exactly your regulation family. His mother had died when he was a kid and he'd been raised by the stepfather who'd adopted him legally when Sam was ten. And, though the man had tried, he really hadn't had much of a knack for being a dad. He'd spent far more time with his insurance business than he had with his son. In fact, the old man had finally had a heart attack and died at his desk just two years ago.

But several months back, a private detective had caught up to Sam to inform him that he was a member of the Fortune family. Now, not only did he have aunts and uncles and cousins, but half brothers and sisters he'd never known about. Still, those relationships were too new, too fragile to count on. He wasn't about to go running to the Fortunes for help. He'd figure a way out of this himself.

It was just going to take a little time.

With the twins down for a nap, Michelle plugged in her laptop and took a seat at the kitchen table, planning to get a little work done. Thanks to the Internet and phone lines, there was really very little she couldn't do away from her desk at home.

First, she went on line to check her Web site for any new e-mails. There were three. The first two were simply questions about the business, but the last was from Miranda Fortune.

Michelle, where are you, girl? Call me.
Miranda

Michelle disconnected from the Internet and picked up the phone. She dialed the number and waited. Finally, on the sixth ring, the phone was snatched up and Miranda's soft Texas voice came on the line. "Hello?"

"Hi Miranda, it's Michelle. I got your e-mail."

"Thank Heaven," the other woman said. "I've been looking for you."

"Why, what's up?"

"Oh, let's see," Miranda said, and Michelle heard the smile in her voice, "I'm getting married in less than a month, I'm having a dinner party for Daniel's business associates next week. My wedding's next month, and my cook just quit. How's your life?"

"Not quite that harried," Michelle admitted, then leaned back in her chair. "But what I meant was, why were you trying to get hold of me?"

"I wanted to tell you not to order that salmon for the wedding dinner." She sighed. "Daniel wants steak."

Michelle smiled into the phone and made a note

on her memo pad. "He's a down-to-the-bone Texan, Miranda. Of course he wants steak."

"I know," Miranda said with a chuckle. "I suppose I should be glad he's not insisting on having the guests rope their own dinner. I swear, the man was born a century too late. He would have been perfectly happy as a cowboy."

"Probably, though I can't picture you as a frontierswoman."

"Oh Lordy, honey, no. Not me, thanks." Miranda took a breath and sighed. "I'm afraid I like the little conveniences." Then she did an abrupt subject change. "So where are you, anyway? I called your house a couple times this morning."

"Actually," Michelle said, standing up and walking to the kitchen, "I'm at Sam's place."

"Sam? My nephew Sam?"

"That's the one."

"Well, honey, do you have something interesting to tell me?"

Michelle cringed a little. "No, I'm just helping him out with the babies."

"But I sent him to a perfectly wonderful agency."

"Apparently the nannies they sent didn't work out."

"Why didn't he say something to me about it?" Hurt colored her voice, and Michelle spoke up quickly.

"I'm sure he didn't want to bother you with it any more."

"He's not a bother, Michelle. He's family."

And she meant it. Miranda had a heart as good as gold. And it didn't matter a damn to her that Sam and the other Fortune heirs had only been discovered a few months ago. Family was family and that's all that mattered.

"I'm sure he knows that Miranda," Michelle said, "but Sam's pretty much of a loner. He always has been."

"Hmm...that's right. You knew Sam years ago, didn't you?"

"Yes, I did."

"Any sparks between you two that I should know about?"

"Sparks?" Michelle asked, remembering the heat that engulfed her every time Sam was anywhere near her. The word *sparks* really didn't describe it. Now maybe the words *forest fire*...oh my.

"Don't play dumb with me, Michelle Guillaire," Miranda teased. "Since there's nothing you want to tell me, how about you come to dinner tomorrow night, and we can talk about the wedding plans?"

"I suppose I could do that."

"Well, good," Miranda said. "And you give those babies a kiss from their Aunt Miranda, all right?"

She hung up then, and Michelle stared at the

phone while the dial tone hummed annoyingly. The other woman was up to something.

The question was, *what exactly?*

And Michelle sure as heck didn't want to be dragged into a discussion about Sam. It wouldn't take long for Miranda to figure out what Michelle had realized only too recently herself.

She was still in love with Sam Pearce.

Hopelessly, helplessly, in love.

Eight

Sam walked into the house that afternoon and stopped dead.

The place looked as if a baby store had exploded in the living room. Stunned, his gaze swept from one item to the next. A single-file twin stroller, two giant stuffed rabbits, one pink and one yellow, a stack of unopened boxes and a mountain of diapers.

"Where the hell did all of this stuff come from?" he asked, though he was alone in the room.

"Well," Michelle's voice floated to him from down the hall, "most of it came from Neiman-Marcus. The rest of it from the Babies Are Our Business store downtown."

"Neiman-Marcus?" Sam repeated, appalled, as he headed for the hall. He accidentally kicked a baby doll and sent it careening into the wall where it lay limply, wailing "Ma-ma" in a tinny voice. Oh, man.

"Yep," she called back, then mumbled, "Come on sweetie, you can do it."

"Do what?" he asked, and stopped in the hallway.

Michelle was crouched down beside the babies, each of whom were sitting in little walkers. Bouncing up and down on the seats, their toes straining for the floor, their hands slapping at the brightly colored rings on the trays in front of them, Beth and Marie were obviously having a great time.

A smile tugged at the corners of his mouth as he watched the twins. Then he shifted his gaze to Michelle and his mouth went dry. Her ponytail was slightly askew, her sweatshirt sported a few splotches of baby food and her proud grin stretched practically from ear to ear.

He'd never seen her look more beautiful.

Something in his chest tightened until it felt as though he was caught in a vise and some unseen hand was cranking it closed. Pain swept through him, carrying slivers of misery through his bloodstream. How had he made it through the last ten years without being able to see her? How could he make it through the next ten minutes without touching her? And why did he still care? Damn it, this shouldn't be so hard.

Ten years ago, she'd ripped his heart right out of his chest and tossed it aside. She'd walked away from everything they'd had together and hadn't even bothered to tell him why. So why in the hell did he still want her so much? Why couldn't his heart understand what his head had finally learned? That whatever he and Michelle had once shared was long gone—buried beneath years of emptiness and a shroud of betrayal.

"Sam? Are you okay?"

He blinked and stared directly into those violet eyes that continued to haunt him nightly.

"Yeah. Yeah," he said, determined to keep his mind from straying where it had no business going anymore. "I'm fine." Watching the kids in their new walkers, he said, "I can't afford Neiman-Marcus. How'd you get this stuff?"

"Gabrielle came over, and we went shopping and—"

He held one hand up in mock surrender. He knew darn well that Miranda's daughter was almost a force of nature. She couldn't be stopped any more than you could hold off a hurricane.

"She said to tell you to consider this stuff a late baby shower."

"Perfect," he muttered. He hadn't wanted to touch the Fortune money he supposedly had coming to him. So instead, one of his cousins had spent money *for* him. And he didn't have a clue as to how he could return any of this stuff without offending Gabrielle.

Families. Geez, this was going to take a lot of getting used to.

But at the moment...he went down on one knee and watched the babies as they headed toward him in fits and starts, the wheels of the walkers scraping along the wood floor. Their small, identical faces were lit from within, joy practically bubbled up around them, and it was impossible not to be touched by it.

"Hey, you two," he said softly, holding his arms out toward the babies, "what've you got there?"

Marie babbled, and Beth giggled and Michelle watched the three of them, heart aching. She shouldn't be torturing herself this way. Yet, she didn't know what else she could do. She had to help Sam take care of these girls, and she couldn't care *for* them and not care *about* them. They'd rolled into her heart as easily as they were rolling down the hall toward the man smiling at them.

And there would be no getting them out of her heart, now. She'd never forget them, she knew. She'd always wonder where they were and how they were. If they were happy. If they were healthy.

And she'd wonder about Sam.

Easing backward, she sat on the floor and drew her knees up, wrapping her arms around them.

Watching the little family come together, Michelle was left where she would always be.

On the outside looking in.

The next night, Sam was standing on the front porch of his aunt's home in Kingston Estates, giving his new daughters a pep talk.

"Now, you two behave yourselves. You don't want Miranda to regret inviting us to dinner, do you?"

They laughed at him, and he didn't know if that was a good sign or a bad one. Stoically, he reached out and pressed the doorbell.

A moment later, the front door swung open.

"Give me one of those sweet babies," Miranda crooned and nearly lunged at Sam. Quickly, she snatched Marie off his hip and cuddled the baby close to her chest, gently jiggling her.

"Ah, Miranda," Sam said, keeping a wary eye on the baby otherwise known as the Spitter, "you might not want to bounce her up and down so much, she just ate and—"

He broke off when Marie, true to form, burped up half her dinner down the front of Miranda's midnight-blue silk shirt. Sam groaned silently. A hell of a first impression on the family, kid. And he silently prayed this wasn't an omen of more disasters to come.

But Miranda wasn't a bit fazed. "Oh, you poor

sweet thing," she whispered, smoothing Marie's soft hair back from her face. "Did you have an upset tummy?"

The little girl smiled and leaned into the woman holding her, and Miranda gave Sam a quick look, apparently reading his expression. "Don't you worry about a thing, darlin'," she said. "Babies do things like that all the time. Besides, it's just a blouse, not the end of the world."

Just a blouse, Sam thought, that probably cost half a week's pay. He didn't know if he'd ever get used to the easy wealth of the family he now belonged to. But Miranda's warmth was hard to ignore.

Sighing, he said, "I'm sorry about that. Here, I'll take her."

"Don't be silly," his aunt answered. "Why don't you go on into the living room and say hello while the baby and I go get cleaned up?"

Without waiting for an agreement from him, Miranda turned on her Ferragamo-clad heel and headed off down the hall, still cooing to Marie.

Beth slapped one little hand against his cheek, and he looked at her, one eyebrow lifted. "You've stopped cryin' all the time, why can't your sister quit erupting every time she eats? And don't you go getting any ideas, all right? One spitter in this family is plenty."

The baby chuckled from deep in her belly, and the

sound brought a smile to his face. "You're gonna charm your way through life, aren't you?"

Then he took a firm grip on the diaper bag that had become an extension of his arm and walked toward the sounds of conversation.

He'd been to Miranda's house in Kingston Estates once or twice before this, but the place always impressed him. Beautiful, elegant, it made him feel like the proverbial bull in a china shop. Not that it was all frills and whatnots, though. The tile floors were polished to a high gleam, arched doorways boasted paintings of flowering vines that almost made you feel as though you were in a garden and there were fresh flowers everywhere. Mexican art hung on the walls alongside paintings done by Texan artists. The whole place reeked of money and good taste while somehow maintaining a cozy, welcoming air.

Still, Sam wasn't used to such high living, and he lived in fear he'd knock over one of the oversized vases or trip and slam into a cabinet holding a collection of Southwestern pottery. Now, with the twins to worry about, he knew he wouldn't be relaxing tonight. He'd have to keep a constant eye on the girls or God knew what they'd get into.

The soft strains of classical guitar music drifted from the stereo and hung on the air, and muted voices became clearer, louder as he neared the living room. And his steps only faltered a bit when he recognized one of those voices as Michelle's.

Frowning, he wondered why she hadn't said anything about coming to Miranda's tonight. But then, he thought, they didn't spend much time talking, did they? Their "no touching" rule had somehow evolved into a "no talking" rule as well.

Last night, she'd left right after the twins had toddled down the hall. This morning, she hadn't said two words to him when she'd arrived, and this evening when he'd come home—the moment he'd walked in the door—she'd picked up her purse and her computer and gone home. He'd almost stopped her. Almost reached out to grab her arm and turn her around, forcing her to look at him. To *see* him. But they'd made an agreement, and it was best for everyone involved if he did his best to stick to it.

No matter what it cost him.

He shouldn't complain, he knew. After all, Michelle had ridden to his rescue, hopping in and taking over when he'd needed help most. And the twins were happy and well taken care of during the day.

But a part of him—a damned traitorous part of him—wanted more. Wanted to talk to her. To hold her. To touch her. To make love with her again. To get her to tell him why she packed up, picked up and walked out on him ten years ago.

He stopped on the threshold of the living room and his gaze instantly swung to Michelle. As if she were the only warm body in the room. As if there were nothing else on this earth worth looking at.

And she made a helluva picture.

She sat on a brown suede couch, one leg curled up beneath her. Her hair was loose and wavy, resting against her cheeks like black velvet, soft and dark. Her skin looked luminous in the light of the fire flickering in the kiva fireplace, and her eyes held the light and the magic of the flames.

As if she sensed his presence, she turned from the woman she was speaking to and looked straight at him. Their eyes met, and, even from across the room, he felt the hard, solid punch of the connection slam straight into his gut.

A moment ticked by, then two. Silence stretched out and became an invisible force in the room. And still they stared only at each other.

"Uh, excuse me?" Riley Sinclair prodded. "Would you two like to be alone?"

"Cut it out, Riley," his wife Emma said, clucking her tongue at him in disapproval.

Michelle tore her gaze away and nervously started plucking at the fall of her denim skirt.

"Come on in, Sam," Justin Bond said from his post behind his wife Heather. "Would you like a drink?"

Sam shook his head as if he were coming up from under water and stepped into the room. He set the diaper bag down and with a nod, said, "Yeah, a beer'd be great right now."

"Coming up." Justin walked across the room toward the bar. Snatching a beer out of the refrigerator, he handed it to Sam as he passed. "Miranda told us you'd be coming by with the babies." He looked confused for a minute then asked, "Where's the other one?"

"Miranda has her. Slight problem."

"Oh, I'll go help," Michelle said instantly and practically leaped off the couch. She kept her head down as she escaped the room, passing within a hairbreadth of him. Sam caught a whiff of her perfume that drifted right down into his soul.

Gritting his teeth, he took a swig of beer and swallowed hard, as he would have a foul-tasting medicine.

It didn't help.

As conversations resumed, Sam bounced Beth on his hip and let his gaze drift across the people gathered in the great room. More family, he thought. Justin Bond and Emma Sinclair were Miranda Fortune's children. She'd given them up for adoption when she was barely more than a kid herself. She'd only recently found them again and now they, too, were getting used to being a part of the Fortune clan. His cousins, Sam thought, with a slight shake of his head.

For a man who'd spent most of his life alone, being inundated with family was a hard thing to get used to. But he was trying.

"So," Sam asked as he eased down onto the floor and set Beth down in front of him between his legs, "what's the occasion? Miranda going to run the wedding plans by all of us?"

Justin and Emma exchanged a glance, and, in that split second, Sam saw the distinct resemblance between them. But then, they were twins, after all. He ran one hand up and down Beth's back and wondered what it must be like for the brother and sister who only recently had discovered each other's existence. He'd seen firsthand the closeness between Beth and Marie and he couldn't imagine anyone splitting the two of them up.

From a distance, the front doorbell sounded and instantly, Emma and Justin stiffened. Nervousness showed clearly on their features, and Sam wondered just what in the hell was going on.

"This is it," Justin murmured.

"What?" Sam asked, but no one answered him.

The adult twins stood together, like a unit, and faced the doorway, waiting.

Miranda came back into the room just then, followed by Michelle with Marie in her arms, and Daniel Smythe. The older man looked as anxious as the two people watching him, and Miranda reached out to take his hand, holding it firmly between both of hers.

"I'm sorry I'm late," Daniel said, his voice gruff as his gaze locked on Justin and Emma. "I meant to get here before everyone else, but something came up and—"

"Daniel," Miranda said softly, "it doesn't matter. All that matters now is that we're all here. Now."

"You're right," the man said with a nod. Then he straightened his shoulders and lifted his chin slightly as if coming to attention.

Sam had the distinct feeling he and Michelle and Riley and Heather were superfluous here. This was something that belonged only to the four people standing only an arm's reach apart. Still, he and the others couldn't look away.

"Justin," Miranda said, "Emma." She paused, pulled in a long, shaky breath and threw an anxious smile at the man she was soon to marry. "I want you to meet your father."

Justin and Emma clasped hands and together faced the man who was their beginning.

Sam held his breath, as did everyone else in the room. Daniel released Miranda's hand and took a single step, then another, toward the children he hadn't even known existed until recently. Tears glimmered in the big man's eyes, and his mouth twisted hard as if he were fighting to hold back a flood of emotion that, if set free, might drown him.

"I never knew," he said, his gaze flicking from one of his children to the other. "If I had only known, I—*we*—might have…" and his voice trailed off. Might-haves didn't matter anymore. There was only the present and what they might build in the future.

Emma was the first one to break. Her gentle heart led her to make precisely the right move. Letting go of her twin's hand, she closed the distance to her father and wordlessly stepped into his embrace. For a long, silent moment, she simply held him and was held. Daniel rested his chin atop her head, and the slow smile that creased his face would've melted a heart of stone. Then Emma stepped back and smiled at him.

"Hello, *Dad*," she said softly.

Daniel sniffed, rubbed one hand across his eyes, then said, "That's sounds almighty good to me, honey." Steeling himself, Daniel then looked at his son and for a long moment, no one spoke.

"Dad?" Justin stepped forward and extended his right hand.

Daniel released a pent-up breath and took Justin's hand in a firm grip before hesitantly pulling the younger man into a brief, hard hug that was as moving in its own way as Emma's silent declaration.

Emotion crowded the room, making the air thick. Then Marie gave a high-pitched squeal that shattered the spell, and Miranda laughed before moving up to the man she'd loved and lost and found again. "Finally," she said, very nearly glowing with the happiness welling inside her, "the four of us are together. As we were always meant to be."

Riley and Heather moved up to join their spouses

and as they all talked together, Sam's gaze shifted to Michelle.

Thirty years, he thought. More than thirty years had passed since Daniel and Miranda had first found each other. And yet, their love had survived. Matured. And had at last brought them full circle.

In less than a month, they'd be married. They'd fought through the old hurts, the old betrayals and found something new. And precious.

And looking at Michelle, Sam wondered.

Nine

A half hour later, Michelle followed Miranda into the kitchen and waited while the other woman opened the huge refrigerator to take out a plate of steaks. Setting the platter down onto the granite-topped cooking island, Miranda shut the fridge then gave Michelle a sheepish smile. Reaching up, she wiped a stray tear from her cheek and said, "I hope we didn't embarrass you."

"No," Michelle lied, "not a bit." But of course she *had* been embarrassed. It was an awkward thing, watching something as private and touching as Daniel's reunion with the children he'd never known. Although at the same time, she'd felt almost *honored* to be a witness to such an a wonderful thing. Michelle couldn't even imagine what Daniel must be feeling. And what about the twins? What must it be like to finally, after a lifetime of wondering, actually meet your father?

Michelle's own life, in comparison, seemed almost boringly normal. Two parents, a house in the suburbs, a "Leave it to Beaver" childhood. In fact, all of this reminiscing had Michelle wanting to call her folks just to touch base. But, as they were on the road in their RV—or as her father called it, the Retirement Vehicle—she'd just call her mom's cell phone later, she thought.

"It wasn't supposed to happen like that. I had this whole night planned," Miranda was saying, and Michelle stopped daydreaming and paid attention. "Daniel was *supposed* to get here early. Before you and Sam," Miranda was saying as she opened and closed cupboards, looking for something. "But naturally, he didn't, and frankly," she said, pausing to glance at Michelle, "I didn't want to make him wait another minute before meeting his children."

"Of course you didn't." Michelle leaned back against the cold countertop and curled her fingers over the edge. Remembering the expression on Daniel's face, she said, "It must be an amazing feeling."

"What?"

"You and Daniel, getting together finally, and then being reunited with your children."

Miranda pulled a long cooking fork out of a drawer and turned around to face her. "You have no idea," she said, her voice soft, wistful. "It's like a dream, and I'm almost afraid I'm going to wake up any minute. If you had told me a year ago that any of this would happen, I would have laughed in your face." She shook her head and laid one hand at the base of her throat where a tasteful gold chain glittered in the overhead light. "But here we stand. Just a month away from getting married and about to have dinner with our kids."

Fresh tears shone in the woman's eyes and Michelle walked to her quickly, wrapping her arms around her friend and giving her a hug.

"Stupid, to keep crying like this," Miranda muttered.

"No it's not," Michelle said, smiling. "It's perfectly understandable. You're happy. And I'm glad to see it."

Miranda chuckled and stepped away. "Thanks, honey. You really are a sweetheart for being so understanding."

Michelle felt the sting of tears in her own eyes and told herself that this was ridiculous. Pretty soon, she and Miranda would be washed out of the kitchen on a river of happy tears. So, to ease the level of emotion off a bit, she quipped, "You know, yesterday you said your cook quit." She glanced at the platter of two-inch-thick steaks. "You're not going to try to cook yourself, are you?"

The ploy worked. Miranda hooted with laughter and waved one hand in the air. "Lordy no, girl. We're just going to throw these steaks on the grill. Nothin' complicated. Heck, Texans are *born* knowing how to barbecue!"

True enough, Michelle thought, smiling as Miranda wandered absently through the kitchen, searching what was clearly unfamiliar territory. But then why wouldn't it be? Miranda had grown up with housekeepers, cooks and drivers. The Fortunes lived in a world apart from the rest of us, Michelle thought. Now, whether Sam was comfortable with it or not, he was one of them. And Michelle wasn't entirely sure what to make of that.

Grabbing up a bottle of barbecue sauce, Miranda said, "All right now, I'm taking these steaks out to Daniel. We'll let the men do the actual cooking. There's just nothing a man likes better than cooking raw meat over an open fire. Must be a caveman thing." She grinned conspiratorially and added, "There are some drinks in the fridge. Why don't you get whatever you and Sam want and come on out?"

"I'll be right there," Michelle assured her, then watched the swinging door slap back and forth through the air after her friend left the room.

Get whatever Sam wants, huh? Well now, that was

the problem, wasn't it? she told herself. She didn't have a clue what it was that Sam wanted.

Sam sat in the chair between the cribs and watched the girls as they slept. A big night, he thought. At least for Daniel and Miranda. Not to mention Justin and Emma.

Maybe it was too late for the four of them to be the kind of family they might have been. But at least they had a chance to know each other. To be a part of each other's lives.

"And that's what counts, isn't it?" he asked aloud in the silent room.

Family. Hell, in the last few months, he'd had more family around than he had his entire life. And though they baffled him on a regular basis, he had to admit, if only to himself, that he kind of liked the feeling of belonging to such a huge family.

But he wasn't really thinking about the Fortunes at all, was he? Nope, his thoughts were centered right where they shouldn't be. On Michelle. If Daniel and Miranda could find their way back to each other after more than thirty years, couldn't he and Michelle do the same after ten?

"Don't be stupid," he told himself sternly. "Nothing has really changed. She walked out on you ten years ago. What's to say she wouldn't do the same damn thing again now?"

Without warning, Michelle's image drifted into focus in his mind as he thought about that. His body went on full alert, and he groaned quietly at the discomfort. He wanted her. Body and soul. His brain constructed the picture of her face, her eyes, locked with his in a room full of people. He'd read all sorts of emotions in those violet depths yet he couldn't be sure if he was seeing them because he wanted to see them or if they were really there.

All he was sure of was that it was only the years of discipline instilled in him by the Marines that had kept him from going to her, pulling her up from her seat and into his arms. He'd wanted her so badly, his whole body had ached with it.

And since the night they'd made love, the wanting had only grown—building on itself until Sam felt as though he'd choke on the need swirling inside. But despite his body's wants, the still-rational corner of his brain warned him to keep his distance. He couldn't risk it. Not again. There was more at stake now. More hearts—more lives—involved than just his and Michelle's. And he wouldn't gamble Beth's and Marie's happiness on the chance that this time things would be different.

Their needs had to come first.

One of the twins sniffed in her sleep, and, drawn out of his thoughts, Sam swiveled his head to look at Marie. Frowning, he wondered if she was getting sick, and from there his mind traveled at light speed. What if one of them did get sick? Seriously sick?

What would he do then? He was a single father. How could he hope to take care of them and manage to keep doing his job to support them? And how was he going to maintain his deployment eligibility for the U.S. Marine Corps? Of course, the twins' parents never thought they'd die too early. No one did.

How in the hell did single mothers do it?

He wasn't entirely alone. He did have people he could lean on in an emergency, though the question of a legal guardian for the children so he could be deployed was still up in the air.

Groaning quietly, Sam closed his eyes. "I don't know yet, girls," he whispered, leaning his head against the back of the chair. "So far, I have way too many questions and far too few answers. But I promise you, I'll think of something. I won't let you down. I won't let your father down."

And listening to the sounds of the twins breathing, Sam fell asleep, racing eagerly toward the dreams that would take him to Michelle.

They settled into a routine that seemed almost cozy. Two weeks passed, every day like the one before. Every morning, Michelle was there, bright and early, laptop in hand. Sam left for work, and she and the girls spent the day together.

When he came home, the scent of dinner cooking always greeted him first, and then there were two smiling little faces, desperately happy to see him. He and Michelle would share a few tense minutes of conversation, and then she'd run from the house as if the hounds of Hell were at her heels.

Two weeks and nothing had changed. And yet, he thought as he walked up the drive toward the front porch, *everything* was changing.

He'd changed. He found himself hurrying to get home. And it wasn't just the girls he was anxious to see.

This no-touching policy was getting harder to honor every day. Every time he saw Michelle, he had the urge to grab her and kiss her and bury himself inside her. What made it even harder was knowing that she felt the same way. He could see it in her eyes. Read it in her expression, her body language.

And her desire fed his until it was a raging thing, caged, yet desperate to break free.

Sam stopped on the porch and paused a moment to enjoy the scent of roasting chicken drifting through the screen door. He heard Michelle's voice as she sang the girls a song. A baby cooed and howled along and he smiled, knowing it was the more outgoing Marie.

The twins' separate and distinct personalities had asserted themselves, and Sam couldn't imagine why he'd had such a time telling them apart at first. The black lettering on the soles of their feet had faded with innumerable baths and the passage of time—

just as the memories of his quieter, lonelier life before them had faded.

He was their father.

The simple realization slipped up on him and slammed into his gut with the force of a huge fist to the midsection.

Dave and Jackie would always be their birth parents, but the twins were Sam's now. He couldn't love them more if they were his own flesh and blood. And he couldn't even imagine his life without them in it.

He reached out, grabbed the door handle and yanked it open, listening to the screech of the hinges as if it was a symphony. That simple, annoying sound meant *home*. A place he'd never really thought to have.

Michelle broke off singing abruptly, and Sam sighed, shaking his head. Now she'd grab up her stuff and race for the door. Well damn it, they were adults. Surely they could manage to keep their damn hormones in check for a few minutes.

"Daddy's home," she said, her voice carrying down the hall to him.

His heart twisted at her words as he headed for the girls' room. *Daddy.*

He stopped on the threshold, and Michelle turned toward him, a half smile on her face. "Hi," she said, and he heard the forced cheerfulness in that one word. "I didn't notice what time it was."

"I'm a little early," he admitted, not bothering to

tell her that he'd come home early on purpose, hoping—hoping for what? he asked himself.

She nodded and pushed herself up from the floor where she'd been sitting alongside the playpen where the girls sat surrounded by plush animals and noise-making toys.

"Well," she said, giving the twins one last smile, "dinner should be ready by now. The girls have already eaten, so I'll—"

"Stay," he blurted before he could keep the word back.

"What?"

"For dinner," Sam finished awkwardly and wondered why in the hell it was suddenly so hard to talk to a woman he knew so intimately. Hell, his hands and mouth had explored every inch of her body. He knew her secrets. Knew her pleasures. Knew everything, he told himself, but why she'd left him.

That still stung, but now wasn't the time to pursue it. If he tried, she'd bolt for the door, and he really didn't want that.

"I don't know," she said, tugging at the hem of the deep-red tunic top she wore over her jeans.

"Why not?" he asked. "You have to eat anyway, and I'm sure you made more than enough. You always do."

"Yeah," she said, "but Sam—"

"Just dinner," he said.

"Just dinner?"

"And maybe some conversation." He reached up and shoved one hand along the side of his head. "For

God's sake, Michelle. Don't you think we can share a meal without lunging at each other across the table?''

Her skin flushed at the mental image, and Sam felt the heat of her reaction from five paces away. Damn, this was strong stuff that lay between them. He'd never known anything like it before. Not with anyone.

''Stay,'' he said again, his voice tight and thick with the river of emotions coursing through him. ''Have dinner with me.''

She met his gaze, and, for a long minute, he thought she would refuse him. But finally, she nodded and said simply, ''All right.''

This all felt too cozy, she thought twenty minutes later as she and Sam sat across the table from each other. Of course, it beat the heck out of sitting at home alone with some microwaveable frozen treat. She cooked for Sam because she enjoyed it. Cooking for herself was just work.

Before her husband had died, she'd taken pleasure in putting a meal together. But since she'd been alone, it hadn't seemed worth the effort.

It worried her a little how much she enjoyed doing the small, everyday tasks for Sam.

To take her mind off of that particular worry, she asked, ''So, sign up any new prospects lately?''

He chuckled and swallowed a bite of chicken before saying, ''Had a real live one today.''

Michelle smiled. ''Tell me.''

"Well," Sam said, leaning his forearms on the table, "this kid liked the idea of wearing a uniform. Said it would get the chicks' attention."

She nodded solemnly, but her lips quirked in a half smile. "Speaking for my fellow chicks, I must say, he has a point."

He lifted one dark eyebrow. "I'll remember that. Anyway," he went on, "this kid wanted the uniform, but he also wanted to make sure we told his Drill Sergeant that he didn't like getting up early."

"You're kidding."

"Nope," Sam said, grinning. "Mr. Military wanted assurances that he wouldn't be expected to do anything until at least nine in the morning."

"Uh-huh."

"Oh," Sam continued, "and he wanted me to put it into his record that he doesn't like walking so he'd rather be assigned to drive a jeep than march."

"You gotta love him," Michelle said, as she imagined Sam's reaction to the would-be recruit.

"Oh, yeah. He was a prime candidate."

"So what did you tell him?"

"I told him if that's the kind of military career he wanted, he should join the Navy, not the Marines."

She laughed with him, and the sound of his laughter washed over her like a soft, pure rain after a drought.

"I've missed this," he said quietly.

Michelle's smile slowly faded as she looked into his green eyes and saw far too much in their depths. She should leave, she knew. Go quickly before she did something stupid like reach out to him, ask to be held, touched, *loved*. But she couldn't leave at this moment any more than she could fly.

"I've missed you too, Sam," she admitted.

"I used to imagine the two of us like this, with a bunch of kids running in and out."

"I know," she said softly. "I always knew how much you wanted a family."

"I promised myself I wouldn't ask this..."

"Then don't," she interrupted him quickly. "Don't look back."

"That's the only place we *can* look, Michelle," he told her softly. "We don't have a present, and you told me ten years ago there was no future for us. *Back* is all we've got."

"Then we don't have anything." She pushed herself up from the table and wasn't the least bit surprised when he stood up, too.

Laying one hand on her forearm, Sam waited until she looked at him before saying, "Don't keep doing that."

"Doing what?"

"Shutting me out."

"Sam, this isn't going to solve anything."

Whatever she might have said was lost when a knock sounded at the door, surprising them both.

Scowling, Sam swiveled his head and glared at the interruption. Then he released her and stalked across the room. Opening the front door, he had a muttered conversation with someone Michelle couldn't see, and, a moment later, he was stepping back into the room holding a business-size envelope.

"What is it?" she asked, moving around the table to walk toward him.

"Registered letter," he said, his gaze never straying from the envelope. "From some lawyer's office." He flicked her a quick glance and she saw the worry glittering in his eyes.

"Open it, Sam."

"Yeah. Open it." He did just that, ripping the creamy white paper and yanking out the letter within. Unfolding it, he read it once, then twice. When he lifted his head to look at her, she watched a string of emotions skate across the surface of his eyes, the strongest of which was pure fury.

"What is it?" she demanded, her heartbeat skittering, her stomach jumping. She reached for the letter even though she knew it was none of her business.

Sam handed it over, and, as she read it for herself, he boiled the contents down into one succinct sentence.

"Dave's parents, the twin's grandparents, are going to try to get custody of the girls."

Ten

"**T**hey can't," Michelle said, her gaze scanning the legal papers before lifting to meet Sam's. "Can they?"

"They seem to think so," he muttered through gritted teeth.

Her head swiveled until she was looking at the shadow-filled hallway leading to the room where two little girls were playing, unaware that their world had just been rocked. Slowly, she backed up and sat down in the closest chair. "I don't believe this," she said softly.

"Me either," he snapped as he paced the room like an animal looking for an escape route.

She felt the anger rippling from him in waves. But along with the rage was a simmering sense of frustration. Worry. And she didn't blame him.

Michelle had seen how close he and the twins had become over the last few weeks. She knew how much those babies meant to him. How much they meant to *her*.

"What are you going to do?"

He shot her a quick look. "Hell, I don't know."

"Well," she said firmly, her fist closing over the papers still clenched in her hand, "you can't let them have the girls."

"Don't you think I know that?" Anger colored his voice, choking it with emotions that had to be racing through him.

"Then you have to have a plan."

"Yeah, but I'll probably need more than ten seconds to come up with one," he told her, sarcasm slashing at her.

"Hey, I'm on your side, remember?" She jumped to her feet, unable to stay seated another minute. She too felt the need to move, to pace. To grab the girls and run far enough that these anonymous grandparents would never be able to find them.

He stopped dead, pulled in a deep breath and blew it out again. "I know," he finally said. "It's just—"

"You need somebody to yell at."

"I guess," he admitted. "But it didn't help."

A reluctant smile curved her lips, and a twinge of

something sharp and sweet tightened around Sam's heart. She was with him on this. She cared about those babies as much as he did. And somehow knowing that made this a little easier to take.

Forgetting all about their agreement, Sam went on instinct and reached for her. Needing something—*someone* to hold onto, he wrapped his arms around her and pressed her tightly to him. She held him, too, her hands smoothing up and down his back, comforting, reassuring. He inhaled the scent of her perfume, drawing it deep within himself as though he was taking a part of her into his soul.

"It'll work out," she said.

"Yeah," he said, wanting to believe her. Resting his chin on top of her head, he stared blankly at the wall across from him.

"We have to think, Sam," she said. "Between the two of us, we'll come up with something."

Sighing, he said, "We'd better."

"They have a strong case," one of the Fortune family lawyers said the next morning after she'd had a chance to look over the papers Sam had given her. An older woman, Sandra Butler had short, neat silver hair, a calm air about her and intelligent blue eyes.

"But Dave and Jackie named *me* guardian," he said, trying to hold onto the temper that seemed constantly to be boiling just beneath the surface. "They didn't expect to die, but they wanted me to have the girls. Not his parents. He told me that they were in their late forties when he was born. Hell, they'll be in their eighties by the time the girls are in their teens.''

''I understand that, Gunnery Sergeant,'' the woman said and took off her gold-rimmed reading glasses. Setting them down on her highly polished desktop, she then folded her hands and smiled at him. It should have been a comforting smile. At least, Sam figured that's how she meant it.

Then she stood up abruptly, walking around the edge of her desk to take the extra seat beside him. Crossing her legs, she tugged the hem of her skirt over her knees and looked at him for a long minute. ''Your late friend's parents are claiming that as a single man, you can't offer the twins a solid home life. They're also saying that your career choice is an unstable one.''

''Unstable?'' He snorted derisively. ''There's a lot less chance of me being fired than some civilian.''

''True,'' she said, still smiling at him. ''Although they're likely to point out that as a Marine, you will be required to leave the children—*alone*—for long periods of time.''

''That'll be taken care of,'' he said quickly. ''I have to have someone named as responsible for them or I can't stay in the Corps. I'm working on it.''

''Good,'' she said nodding, ''the sooner the better.''

"I know."

"It's a shame you're not married," she mused to herself. "Even in this day and age, people prefer to see children in a traditional home."

"Married?" he repeated.

"That would be best," she said softly, "and it would take care of the problem of who would be responsible for the children while you're deployed."

Yeah, it would, he thought, his mind racing even as the lawyer kept talking.

"And the fact that you're an heir to the Fortune family will certainly bear some weight in what could be an ugly custody battle."

That caught his attention and he stiffened slightly. "This doesn't involve the Fortunes," he said. "This is between me and Dave's folks."

Ms. Butler shook her head. "Don't be foolish, Gunnery Sergeant. If you want those children, then you shouldn't be afraid to use anything you can to help your situation."

"I'm not afraid, ma'am," he said, stiffening even at the suggestion.

"Of course not," she agreed, her tone placating. "All I'm saying is, it would be best if we faced the grandparents with as strong a case as possible."

"I'm all for that."

"Then for heaven's sake, accept the fact that the Fortune family name will carry a lot of weight with any judge."

It went against the grain. He was a man who fought his own battles. Stood up for himself. Hell, it was a measure of his desperation that he'd called Ryan Fortune and asked for assistance in finding an attorney. Now that he had that attorney, he'd be a fool not to listen to her advice, wouldn't he? He simply wasn't used to the idea of running for help, and it didn't sit well at all knowing that she was right.

If the girls were important to him, he had to be willing to do whatever was necessary to keep them. After all, why go into a battle with no ammunition? Nodding to himself, Sam made up his mind. He'd use whatever he had to to win this. The attorney. The Fortunes. He had to think of this coming fight as he would a military mission. Gather his forces, devise a plan, then make a stand.

And as that decision was made, an idea took root in his mind. An idea that was so nuts, it just might work.

"Married?" Michelle asked, sure she hadn't heard him right. "You want us to get *married?*"

"Yeah," Sam said tightly. "And it has to be soon."

He'd thought about this all morning, and it was the only solution that made sense. "Married, I'll probably get custody of the babies. Plus, I'm covered as far as the Corps goes—I have to have someone for the kids to stay with when I'm deployed." It hadn't been easy, proposing to the woman who'd already turned down a marriage proposal from him. But damn it, it was all he could think of. He needed this settled and settled quickly.

"This is nuts," she said, and grabbed up her purse from the couch.

"It's not nuts," he snapped. "It's desperation."

She slanted a look at him and he saw the shimmer of hurt in her eyes. But he couldn't afford to be swayed. And he couldn't afford to give up. Not this time.

"Look," he said, reaching out to lay one hand on her forearm, "think of it as a business proposition."

"Business?"

"Yeah." Talking fast now, he went on, laying it all out for her exactly as it had come to him at the lawyer's office. "Call it a marriage of convenience. I need a wife. And you're the only one I can marry and have everyone convinced it's the real deal. The lawyer thinks that if I'm married and have the weight of the Fortune family behind me, we can settle this custody issue without even going to trial." Reaching up, Sam shoved both hands along the sides of his head. "And damn it, I'm *not* going to lose those girls."

"But marriage, Sam?"

"It's the only way." His gaze snapped to hers. "You turned me down once before..."

She flinched, but he had to ignore it.

"This time it's different. It'll be a marriage in name only. This time it's not about my love for you, but about *our* love for those kids."

She bit down hard on her bottom lip and her eyes softened.

"I know you love them too, Michelle," he said, his voice dropping to a whisper. "Help me keep 'em safe."

Michelle looked into those deep-green eyes of his and knew she was going to say yes. How could she say anything else? She'd said no once before and it had cost her everything that had mattered to her. Now, it seemed as though life was handing her a second chance. Another grab at the brass ring. She'd be a fool to turn away from it.

Besides, she reasoned, the situation was different now, wasn't it? He already had the family he'd craved. She could help him raise the children they never could have had together. And maybe, with time, he would understand why she'd left him so long ago, and, instead of concentrating on old hurts, they could create a future together.

But should she tell him about William? No, she thought. Not now. Later. Because a small voice in the back of her mind worried that if he knew she'd married someone else after turning him down, he just might find a different way to solve his current problem. And she didn't want that.

He was waiting. His body tight, his features tense, he watched her, studying her face, hoping for a sign.

Michelle pulled in a deep, steadying breath and nodding, said, "All right, Sam. I will marry you."

As he gave her a slow, relieved smile, she hoped to high heaven she was doing the right thing.

They'd wanted a small, simple ceremony. But Miranda wouldn't hear of it. The poor woman was so pleased at the idea of her friend marrying her nephew, she arranged for the marriage to take place on the Double Crown Ranch, the Fortune family home. Since Michelle and Sam wanted this marriage to look as real as possible to the outside world, they'd had to agree.

So, only two weeks after Sam's sudden proposal, Michelle found herself wearing daisies in her hair and a long-sleeved, forest-green gown, standing in front of the huge stone fireplace in Ryan's living room. Miranda, as her matron of honor, delicately sniffled into a lace-edged hanky and from somewhere behind the couple, the twins kept up a stream of babbling. The only ones missing were Michelle's parents, who, according to their most recent phone call, were somewhere in New Hampshire. But they'd sent their best wishes and promised to make Texas their next destination.

A small cluster of friends and family surrounded Sam and Michelle as they said their vows. Justin, the best man, handed Sam the ring, and, as he slid the simple gold band onto Michelle's finger, the deed was done. For better or worse, they were finally married.

"You may kiss the bride," the minister said, grinning at Sam like a proud papa.

"Yes sir," he answered and, gorgeous in his dress blues uniform, turned toward her and gave her a small, private smile. Then dipping his head, he claimed the traditional kiss.

Their lips met briefly, but, as if that simple touch had stirred sleeping embers, fire leaped up between them and Sam deepened that kiss. Taking, giving, tasting, he crushed her to him in a powerful embrace, slanting his mouth atop hers, he surrendered to a need that had been too long denied. He could have stayed like that forever, and might have, if Ryan hadn't stepped up behind him and clapped him on the back. "Come on, nephew," he said, laughing, "let her come up for air and kiss some of your good-lookin' relatives!"

Everyone laughed, and Sam reluctantly broke the kiss. As he lifted his head, he looked down into Michelle's eyes and saw the same passion, the same need he felt, shining in those violet depths. And he was shaken. He'd had every intention of keeping this a business arrangement. But now, now he wasn't sure where they stood. They were married, but would it be a real marriage? Would he be able to put the mistrust behind him? Could he ever let himself love her the way he had before?

But those questions went unanswered as he and Michelle were torn apart by excited wedding guests. One person after another came up to him, wishing him well and offering congratulations on his sudden marriage. His gaze followed Michelle around the room as his new family welcomed her into the Fortune clan.

"You're a lucky man," a voice said right beside him.

He glanced at Miranda and smiled. She looked beautiful, as usual. "Yeah," he said, "I guess I am."

She threaded her arm through the crook of his and gave his shoulder a brief pat. "No guessing about it," she said, following his gaze to look at Michelle, smiling at something Gabrielle had said. "I knew just by looking at the two of you together at dinner the other night that this was coming."

Sam chuckled to himself. "Is that right?"

"Oh goodness yes," she said. "You know, I had nothing against Michelle's first husband, but he was far too old for her. Of course, I'd never say so to her."

First husband?

The roaring in his ears almost drowned out Miranda's voice. Michelle had been married before? She'd turned him down and then married someone *else?* His chest tightened until he wasn't at all sure he'd be able to draw a breath, but somehow he forced himself to ask quietly, "She wasn't happy?"

"Oh, she'd say she was," Miranda said thoughtfully. "But, no, I'd say not. And when William died several years ago, Michelle practically became a hermit." She turned her face up to his and grinned. "You rescued her. That's your Fortune blood showing."

"Must be," he said idly, though his insides were churning. Why hadn't she told him? he thought.

"Now," Miranda was saying, "don't you feel like you have to stick around here for long. The cabin is all set for your honeymoon night and the girls will be fine with me."

He nodded, remembering that they'd agreed to a night's stay in the cabin on the Fortune property. Wanting to make this marriage look as real as possible, they couldn't very well turn it down.

Miranda drifted off into the crowd, leaving Sam alone with thoughts that crowded his mind. Anger warred with the desire within, and even he wasn't sure which of the two emotions was the stronger at the moment. All he knew for sure was he had to get Michelle alone. Soon.

Walking through the still night toward the cabin, Michelle glanced down at her left hand and stared briefly at the gold ring glittering in the moonlight. Night birds called in the distance and a soft, cold wind whipped across the land to dance around her and Sam. She was married. To the man she'd loved for what seemed forever.

And yet—she slanted a look up at him—her groom didn't appear to be the picture of a happy man. Heck, he'd hardly said two words to her since the ceremony. But then, the marriage was only real to everyone else. For the two of them, nothing would change except her address.

A light shone from the window of their honeymoon cabin, welcoming them in from the darkness. And she couldn't help wishing that things were different. That they were about to embark on a *real* wedding night.

Sam opened the door and stepped back to allow her inside first. Michelle walked into the room and her breath caught at the beauty of the place. A simple log cabin, it had been outfitted with overstuffed furniture, throw pillows and a handmade rug. A fire burned cheerily in the hearth and on a small table, a bottle of champagne sat in a silver ice bucket beside two crystal flutes. Fresh flowers scented the warm air with the delicate aroma of hot-house roses and lavender. Through the open doorway off the short hall, Michelle saw the old four-poster bed, piled high with downy quilts and feather pillows. A seductive scene, ready and waiting.

A curl of desire unwound in the pit of her stomach and sent shaky tendrils to every inch of her body.

Her knees wobbled, her mouth dried up and a soft, throbbing ache settled low inside her. She sucked in a gulp of air, hoping to steady herself and found she really needed it when Sam said suddenly, "Tell me about William."

He reached up and snatched his dress cover off his head before flinging it, Frisbee-like, across the room. Sam had held the anger, the sense of betrayal, in check as long as he could. Now he would have the answers she'd denied him for years.

Michelle spun around to look at him, stunned surprise etched onto her features. "William?" she asked breathlessly.

"Yeah," he prompted and heard the growl in his own voice. "You know. Your *first* husband?"

"Oh God."

Thumbing the brass buttons on his tunic free, he said tightly, "Miranda happened to mention that you hadn't seemed happy with your first husband, poor dead William. And she hoped you'd be happier with me."

"I should have told you," she whispered almost to herself and sank down into a half-sitting position on the back of the brightly flowered couch.

"Yeah, you should have." Shrugging out of his jacket, he asked, "So when exactly did you marry him? Right after you broke up with me?"

She shook her head and brushed away a stray tear

that threatened to slip into Sam's heart. But he wouldn't be swayed by her tears. Couldn't be.

"About a year later," she said.

"Wow, a whole year." It had been *two* years before she'd stopped appearing nightly in his dreams. Apparently, he was a lot easier to get over than she'd been.

She flicked him a quick glance, then looked away again. "He was much older than me. A kind man. Gentle. He—"

"I don't want to hear about Saint William," he snapped.

"Then what do you want?" she asked, standing up to face him.

"I want to know why you could marry him, but you couldn't marry me." Sam grabbed her upper arms and pulled her close. "What was it?" he demanded. "I have a right to know. I *need* to know why you tossed me aside and married some guy old enough to be your father."

She yanked free of him, tossed her hair back out of her face and glared into his eyes. "Because *he* didn't want children," she said. "He'd already raised a family. He didn't care that I—"

"That you what?"

"That I can't have children," she said tightly.

Stunned, Sam only gaped at her for a long minute. Then a harsh, humorless laugh shot from his throat and he slapped one hand to his forehead. "And you thought I *would* care? You thought that would matter to me?''

''You always wanted kids,'' she said, arguing hotly in her own defense. ''You used to talk about it all the time. And when I found out I couldn't give you children, I—''

''—kicked me out of your life?'' he finished for her.

''Let you go,'' she corrected. ''For your sake.''

''Oh,'' he said, nodding. ''Sure, that makes sense. You ripped out my heart for my own good.''

''Do you think it was easy for me? Do you think I enjoyed watching you walk out of my life?''

He leaned in close, eyes narrowed, ''You did it, easy or not. You didn't give me a vote. Didn't trust me. You walked out.''

''For you,'' she shouted at him. ''So you could find someone else. Have the family you always wanted.''

She actually believed what she was saying, he thought wildly. For God's sake, she'd actually convinced herself that he'd rather have kids with someone else than have her. And she'd thrown away the life they might have had for *this?*

''That is the dumbest thing I have ever heard.''

She smacked him, surprising them both.

''Don't you say that,'' she said. ''I did what I had to.''

He lifted one hand to his stinging right cheek and worked his jaw. "You never heard of adoption?"

"Yes, but—"

"We could have had kids together, Michelle. They didn't have to be born from us to be ours. Don't you think the way we feel about the twins proves that? Jesus," he shouted, "*I* was adopted!"

She rubbed her hands up and down her forearms and muttered to herself. "I did the right thing. I know I did. You wouldn't have wanted to stay with me."

"But you'll never be sure now, will you?" The wasted years rose up in his mind, and he wanted to rage in fury for all they'd lost. But it wouldn't accomplish a damn thing. Ten years that they might have had together were gone.

She lifted her chin and looked at him through tear-washed eyes. "Sam—"

"You threw it away," he said, and moved in close to her again. Planting both hands on her shoulders, he drew her in tight against him until she had to tip her head back to look into his eyes. "You made the decision for both of us and cheated us out of a lifetime."

Her breath hitched, and another tear rolled along her cheek and straight into his heart.

Gritting his teeth, he tightened his hold on her and asked, "Did you find what we had with William? Did he make you feel this?" He took her mouth like a full-scale assault. He parted her lips with his tongue, pushing into her warmth, demanding that she give as well as take. Demanding that she acknowledge all they shared. All they'd missed. Her arms came around him and held on tightly. She opened to him, bending into his body, leaning against him as she gave herself up to the emotions churning between them. And when, an eternity later, he raised his head and looked down at her, his last question still evident in his eyes, she shook her head.

"It's you, Sam. Only you."

And for tonight, that was enough.

Eleven

He didn't care about tomorrow. The future could take care of itself. For tonight, for this moment, all he wanted was here, in his arms.

Without a word, Sam scooped her up and carried her into the bedroom. She clung to him, and he felt the thundering pounding of her heart racing in tandem with his. Setting her on her feet, he quickly stripped out of his uniform, then helped her as she tried unsuccessfully to tug at the narrow zipper running down the back of her dress.

As he slid it free, inch by inch, exposing the line of her back to his hungry gaze, Sam gave into the need to taste her. He pushed the dress down off her shoulders and turned her in his hands until she was facing him. Then he bent his head and took one of her nipples into his mouth. His lips and tongue tortured her gently, hungrily as his hands explored her curves. His fingers moved across her skin, and she held onto him tightly, bending, twisting in his grasp, moving into him, silently offering him more. More.

"Sam, Sam I need—"

He knew just what she needed because he needed the same thing. Fire bubbled within him, and when he laid her back onto the bed, he didn't give her a chance to think. He didn't want either of them to think. Not now. Not at this moment. This moment was for the fire. For the want and hunger they'd both lived with for ten years.

His mouth, fast and urgent, ravished every inch of her. His teeth tugged at one rigid nipple, and he felt and tasted the quick, staccato beat of her heart. The rhythm pushed him on, and he went faster, harder, deeper. His fingers dipped expertly inside her, and he felt her damp heat welcome him home.

Her hips arched into his palm and he gave her what she wanted, what they both wanted. In and out, his fingers moved within her, his thumb rubbing the bud of her sex, taking her just to the edge of completion before pulling back, making her tremble with the need for release. And as his hands worked her flesh below, his mouth took her breasts, one after the other, biting, sucking, licking, he drove her higher, faster than she'd ever been before.

Time faded away as he claimed the woman who should have been his.

Michelle planted her feet on the bed and moved into him. Her fists clutched at the bedsheets, looking for purchase as her world rocked and trembled around her. She couldn't think. Could hardly breathe. His mouth. His hands. Everywhere at once. Her body screamed for release even as the tension inside her mounted. Only him, she thought wildly. Her insides tightened, coiling into a hot ball of need. Want. Only Sam could do this to her. For her. She made a grab for him, but her hand dropped limply off his shoulder as an overwhelming, rippling climax began deep inside her.

She thought she might have screamed when the first wave hit her hard, but she couldn't be sure. Her hips rocked, her back arched and she tipped her head into the mattress as pulse after pulse of pure, undiluted pleasure swept over her. And, before the last tremor had coursed through her body, he was there again. Slipping inside her. Making his body a part of her. An extension of her heart. Her soul. He thrust himself home, deeply, completely. And as he moved against her, she squirmed, hoping to take him even deeper, to somehow hold him so far inside herself that he would never be able to leave. That in some way, they would always be joined, even when they were apart.

Then her mind went blank as the eruption within began again. Her already sensitized body quivered as he took her up that peak one more time. He pushed her, driving them both with a frenzied need that demanded to be fed.

"Look at me," he said tightly, and Michelle's eyes flew open. Her gaze blurred with passion, she stared into his green eyes as he rocked against her, filling her, taking all of those lonely, empty corners and banishing them forever. "See me," he said, "only me," and one hand cupped her breast, his clever fingers tweaking the nipple, teasing her still as he pushed her toward completion. Her body bucked, arched and she cried out as another wave of delight washed over her. And before it was finished, he whispered, "Take me," and lowered his head to ravage her mouth as he emptied himself into her.

A few minutes later, when she was sure she could speak without her voice cracking, Michelle said softly, "Sam, I want you to know—"

"Don't," he told her, cutting her off neatly.

"Don't what?" she asked, turning her head on the pillow to look at him.

He sat up on the edge of the bed, then pushed himself to his feet and walked naked to the lace-covered window. Pulling the sheer curtain aside, he stared out at the night. "Don't say anything."

Damn it, this changed nothing. The sex had always been incredible. But it wasn't enough to make him forget all she'd cheated them out of. It wasn't enough to ease the anger still churning inside him.

Moonlight spilled into the room like molten silver. He turned his head to look at her and the soft light surrounded him, bathing his body in an otherworldly glow.

"Sam, we have to talk."

He laughed shortly and shook his head. "How long have I been saying that to you?" He reached up and shoved both hands along the sides of his head.

She watched the muscles of his chest stretch and ripple and her mouth went dry with a renewed rush of desire. How could it be so strong? How could she want him more every time?

"We've talked enough tonight," he said finally, and she heard the rumble of banked anger in his voice.

"But—"

"You *married* someone else, damn it!"

Michelle flinched and bit down hard on her bottom lip.

"You were gone. I was alone and—"

He slapped one hand to his chest. "I was alone, too. But I didn't rush right out and marry the first woman I stumbled across."

"I didn't 'stumble' across William," she said, defending herself and her decision. "It was a year after we'd split up."

He threw his arms wide and let them fall to his sides again. "Imagine! A whole year!"

His sarcasm slashed at her and Michelle grabbed a blanket off the bed and wrapped herself up in it. "Why are you doing this?"

"Me? *I'm* doing this?"

"Yes," she said, scooting off the bed to face him. "This is all in the past, why can't you let it go?"

"I told you before, the past is all we have."

"It doesn't have to be."

"You lied to me," he said, staring down into her eyes.

"I never did."

"You didn't tell me the truth. Same thing."

True. She had no argument for that. "I did what I thought was right."

He snorted a choked-off laugh. "It worked out great, didn't it?"

She flushed and was grateful it was too dark for him to see it. Strange how their positions had reversed. But now, while her body was still humming from their lovemaking, she wanted him to know that she'd never loved anyone the way she loved him. She needed him to understand that the decision she'd made at twenty-one had been made out of love. If she'd been wrong, well, she too had paid for the mistake.

So before she could lose her nerve, she said simply, "I never wanted to hurt you." Reaching out, she lifted one hand to his chest and felt the thundering, rapid beat of his heart. "I was trying to step aside, so you could find someone else. Someone to give you the family you always wanted. Don't you see that I paid for that decision as much as you did?"

"All I wanted was you," he said softly, and something tight and sweet squeezed Michelle's heart.

There was only one thing left to say. Words she'd waited ten long years to speak. "I love you, Sam. I always have."

He groaned. "Michelle—"

He lifted one hand and scooped her hair back from her face before cupping her cheek briefly. Then he let his hand fall back to his side and shook his head. "But you didn't *talk* to me," he said. "You didn't trust me—or our love—enough to tell me the truth."

"I wanted to."

"But you didn't," he said again, and there was steel in his tone. "When things got rough, you split. You turned tail and ran."

Michelle nodded jerkily. "Okay, maybe I *did* take the coward's way out. I don't know anymore. But you know, *you* weren't completely innocent either."

"Me?" Clearly astounded, he just stared at her.

"Yeah. You say you loved me desperately, but you let me go."

"You sent me away!"

"And you *went!*"

His jaw tightened and his eyes narrowed. "You didn't leave me much, Michelle. But I had *some* pride. I wasn't going to chase you down when you didn't want me."

Michelle sighed. "I *always* wanted you. But God, Sam, I was so young." She swallowed hard. "And, I was...afraid."

"Of what?"

"I thought that when you found out I couldn't have children, you'd reject me. So I rejected you first."

His head dropped back on his neck. "Ahh, Michelle."

"I can't change what I did," she told him. "I can't go back in time and give us back all we lost. Damn it, Sam, I was a kid. I made a mistake. What's your excuse?"

"What the hell does that mean?"

"It means," Michelle snapped, feeling an ember of anger kick in, "that you're willing to throw everything we *could* have together away out of misplaced pride. You don't even want to try." She took a breath, levelled out her voice and added, "Things are different now."

"Yeah, they are," he said, and swallowed hard.

"It's not just me anymore. I have the twins to think about now."

"I know that, and I want to—"

"And I can't run the risk of you hurting them."

She stopped and eased back from him. Watching him, Michelle felt that ball of ice grow and blossom until it threatened to choke off her air completely. Tears filled her eyes, but she blinked them back. She wouldn't cry. "You think I'd hurt those babies?"

"Not intentionally."

"What are you saying?"

He inhaled sharply and blew the air out again in a rush. "I'm saying that I won't risk loving you again."

The ice inside her cracked, fractured and splintered throughout her body, sending cold shards of pain shooting throughout her bloodstream. Only moments ago, she'd had such hope. She'd felt their souls touch. And now, he was further away from her than ever.

Shaking his head, he looked into her eyes and continued, his voice softer now, but no less determined. "I know you love the girls. And now I know they represent your chance at motherhood..."

Stung, she said, "I didn't marry you to *get* the babies." Planting both hands on his bare chest she shoved him hard enough to back him up a step or two. "You son of a bitch. How can you even say that to me? You know me better than that."

"Yeah," he admitted. "I do. Maybe you didn't do it consciously, but either way, I think it's best if we kept this marriage what it was supposed to be. A business arrangement."

How lonely that sounded now. How empty. "And what was that?" she asked, waving one hand at the rumpled bed behind them. "A *merger?*"

"A mistake," he said simply.

"You didn't think so a minute ago," she reminded him.

"It didn't change anything, Michelle."

She was cold. Cold right down to her bones. Wrapping the blanket more tightly around her in a futile attempt at warmth, she asked, "Do we stay married, then?"

"Yes," he said, "if it's all right with you. At least until I've got this custody thing worked out."

How sad this all was, she thought, anger dying away to lie in a cold heap in her chest. A day that had begun so beautifully was ending with such misery. But she'd had her chance with Sam ten years before. And apparently, despite what she might have thought, Fate only gave you one shot at the brass ring. If you missed it, it was your tough luck.

"Of course," she said dully, letting go of her dreams. "Whatever you need." Wrapped in that quilt, she had a feeling that no amount of blankets would be able to chase away the cold gripping her now.

"Thank—"

She held up one hand. "Don't thank me." Her voice quivered, and she gulped in air like a landed trout. "For heaven's sake, please don't thank me." Her back teeth ground together as she added, "You know...this is all about your pride."

"What?"

"You're the one holding onto the past, Sam. You're the one who's throwing the future away this time." She tightened the blanket around her and lifted her chin. "We could have had it all, that's what's so sad about this. I love you, Sam, I will till I die." Her voice broke despite her efforts, and even seeing his shoulders droop a bit wasn't enough to stop her from saying the rest of what had to be said. "You're living in a love from ten years ago. I'm living in a love that's right now." And before she could embarrass herself further, she stalked across the room. At the threshold though, she paused for one last shot. "War's over, Marine. Congratulations. You won." Then she left without looking back.

So she never saw the pain on his face or the misery in his eyes as he watched her go.

The next few days passed in a fog of unspoken pain.

Sam did his job, but his heart wasn't in it. Why in the hell would he care if some kid joined the Corps or not when all he could think of was that his life was falling apart?

But being at home was no easier. He stared across the bare, winter-brown lawn at Michelle and the girls. Michelle laughed into the breeze and grinned at the twins as they clapped their little hands in sheer joy. Their laughter sweetened the crisp air and clutched at Sam's heart.

He—*they*—could have so much. And yet, a part of him just couldn't let go of the past, despite the fact that he could hear Michelle's voice accusing him of that very thing. Maybe she was right, he thought. But how was a man supposed to forget that the woman he'd once loved more than his next breath had sent him away? And what was to keep her from doing it again?

"Sam!"

Michelle's voice yanked him out of his thoughts. He dropped the rake and took a step before he realized that she didn't need help. She wanted him to look.

One of the twins…impossible to tell which one from this distance…was standing up under her own steam. And as he watched, pride swelling inside him, that tiny girl took one step, then two, then plopped down hard on her diapered bottom.

"That's wonderful, Bethie," Michelle cooed as she picked the baby up, and he heard the affection, the love in her voice.

Sam loped across the yard, reaching his little group of females in a few easy strides. He went down on one knee beside Michelle and Beth, pausing long enough to scoop up Marie and hold her close. Then he stared into those tiny identical faces, framed by the hoods of their bright pink jackets before shifting his gaze to Michelle's.

"Wasn't she amazing?"

"Yeah," he said, staring into her eyes, loving the way her face lit up in pride and love for the girls. "Amazing."

Michelle's heart did a slow roll in her chest, and she wished, desperately, that things were different. But they weren't. They never would be. Sam had made his choice. He'd shut her out as effectively as she had him ten years before. And it would be better for her if she just accepted what was. Starting now.

She handed Beth to Sam and stood up, her empty arms aching as deeply as her heart. "I'll just leave you and the girls alone for a few minutes. This is really a *family* time."

"Michelle..."

She shook her head and swallowed the knot of misery in her throat. Then with carefully measured steps, she turned and headed back to the house, leaving her heart behind her.

Sam watched her go, and, though his arms were full of laughing babies, his heart—his *soul* felt empty.

Three weeks later

Time crawled past, measured in long, tension-filled days. Life in their little house had become almost unbearably polite. Michelle took care of the kids and the house just as always. She made dinner and ran her business and managed to do everything she always had, with one huge exception. She never spoke to Sam. Never looked him in the eye. And God, he missed her. Especially during the even longer, sleepless nights. This was killing him, blast it. Sam rubbed his eyes with his fingertips and told himself he was being a damn fool.

But the fact that he knew that didn't change a thing.

Standing in a corner of Miranda's living room, he watched members of the Fortune family running around like crazy. Apparently, there were plenty of last-minute wedding tasks to be accomplished, and only a few more minutes in which to do them. Guests mingled, wandering through the house, chatting and sipping on the champagne Ryan had provided for his sister's wedding.

And Sam watched it all, a man apart from the festivities. He caught a glimpse of Michelle, smiling up at Kane Fortune, and he wondered if it was only he who noticed the strain around her eyes or that her smile looked forced. Everything inside him told him to cross the floor. Go to her. Talk to her. But an instant later, she was off again, weaving her way in and out of the crowd, keeping an eye on the "event" she'd planned so carefully.

A tug on his slacks drew his gaze down to where Beth was pulling herself up onto her toes by using him to keep herself steady. He smiled softly and realized that she and her sister were counting on him to keep them both safe. To keep their whole world steady. They'd already suffered a loss no kid should have to endure. He'd be damned if he risked their happiness again.

But, a voice in the back of his mind whispered, *is Michelle really a risk?* Or was he using the kids as an excuse to keep his own heart safe from another bruising?

He shook his head and looked down to where Marie was now following her sister's example on his other pant leg. Both girls swayed, wobbled and grinned up at him and he smiled, despite the turmoil inside. "You two think I'm an idiot, don't you?" he asked, then sighed impatiently. "Maybe I am. Hell, a man can't really think if he's not sleeping," he said, though he doubted either one of them was interested.

"I think I have something that will help with that," a woman said from beside him.

Sandra Butler fairly beamed at him as she held out a manila envelope.

"What's this?" he asked, his gaze flicking from

the envelope to the lawyer's satisfied smile and back again.

"These, Gunnery Sergeant," she said, "are the custody papers."

"What?" Hope leaped up inside him. He grabbed the envelope, tore it open and pulled out the papers inside. He scanned the legalese quickly, then lifted his gaze to her again. "You're serious? It's settled?"

"Signed, sealed and delivered," she said, and snagged a crystal flute of champagne from a passing tray. Taking a sip, she said, "The grandparents are willing to let you have custody as long as they can visit the children."

"Visit?" he repeated, glancing down at the two little girls who were now officially his. "Hell, *of course* they can visit," he said, feeling the iron band around his chest that had been such a part of him for so long loosen slightly. "They're the twins' grandparents."

"I thought you'd see things that way," Sandra said with another smile. "Now," she said, letting her gaze trail across the crowd, "I think I'll go get a good seat for the ceremony."

As she turned to leave, Sam's voice stopped her.

"Ms. Butler?"

"Yes?" she asked, watching him.

He shrugged helplessly. "I don't know how to thank you."

"You just did," she assured him and moved off into the crowd.

Alone again, Sam ignored the people drifting out to the terrace and bent down to pick up the girls. Scooping them up, he held them tightly to his chest and gritted his teeth to keep from squeezing them too hard. "You're safe," he whispered. "And you'll stay safe. I swear it."

"Sam?" Michelle's voice. From close by. "Sam, what are you doing? You're going to crush the babies."

His head whipped up, his gaze locking with hers. She saw the sheen of tears in his eyes, and her heart stopped. Something had to be horribly wrong. Nothing less than a tragedy could bring a man like Sam to tears. Fear prodded her heart into a thundering rhythm, pounding frantically against her rib cage.

"What is it?" she demanded, snatching Beth from his arms and holding her close, needing to feel the solid warmth of the baby in her arms. "What's happened?"

"I got custody," he said, and she heard the disbelief in his voice.

A strange tangle of mixed emotions twisted inside Michelle like the tattered threads of an unraveling tapestry, and, in a matter of seconds, she felt them all. Joy, misery, disappointment. He had custody and the girls would be cared for, but now that Sam had the girls, he wouldn't need her, would he?

Head spinning, she pressed a kiss onto Beth's cheek, inhaling the soft, sweet scent of baby and looked up into Sam's green eyes. They'd had three weeks to talk, to bridge the chasm that lay between them, and they hadn't been able to manage it. Of course, the fact that she'd been ignoring him hadn't helped any. She'd lain awake every night, listening to the sounds of him wandering through the house, checking on the girls, pausing at her bedroom door before moving off into the darkness. And she'd cried her tears in the silence, mourning his loss for the second time in her life.

Now, it was too late. She knew it. She felt it and had only a moment or two before the wedding ceremony to let him know it, too. There was no point in pretending differently. Not anymore.

"That's wonderful, Sam," she said, squeezing each word past the knot in her throat. "I'm happy for all three of you."

He stared at her as if he could hear the goodbye in her voice. "What are you saying?" he asked, hitching Marie higher in his arms.

Michelle shook her head and handed him Beth, her hand lingering just a bit longer than necessary on the baby's back. When Marie reached out for her, Michelle's heart broke a little more, but she took a step back and folded her hands behind her back to keep from reaching for the child.

"I'm only saying what we both know is true," she

said, her voice shaking a little. "We only got married so you could get the girls." Her bottom lip quivered, but she kept talking, determined to say it while she still could. "Now that you have custody, you don't need me. Even divorced, I can be their guardian when you deploy."

"Michelle—"

"You don't need me here," she repeated, more firmly this time. "So I'll move out tomorrow. File for divorce."

"Divorce?" He took a step toward her, but Michelle shook her head and backed up again.

"Come on, you two," Riley Sinclair called out on his way to the terrace. "The wedding's about to start."

"Coming," Michelle answered, keeping her gaze locked with Sam's a moment or two longer. And as she turned to join the crowd outside, she whispered, "Goodbye, Sam."

Twelve

Sam hadn't had a moment alone with Michelle since she'd walked away from him just before the ceremony. Busy with the wedding guests and dealing with the caterers, she seemed to be everywhere but wherever he happened to be.

The entire Fortune clan had gathered for Miranda and Daniel's wedding, and all around him people were celebrating. Even Leeza Kovars was here somewhere. He'd seen her earlier, looking as though she was having a great time. Sam wondered about her for a long minute and tried to understand why the woman would stay around when she so obviously wasn't wanted.

Then he put Leeza out of his mind to focus on more pleasant things. His gaze shifted over the crowd. Lily hardly left her husband Ryan's side, as though she couldn't really believe that he'd survived the poisoning attempt and was now healthy again. The "lost heirs" as Sam and the other newly discovered Fortunes were called, had settled right in with their extended family. Riley and Emma were dancing on the terrace while Holly and Guy Blackwolf helped Tara and Jonas Goodfellow entertain all of the babies. Ryan's new-found son, Nico Tan-efi looked every inch the royal sheik as he danced with his bride, Esma Bakkar. Miranda and Daniel strolled through the crowd, hand in hand, as if they couldn't bear not to be touching. Gabrielle and Wyatt Grayhawk were huddled in a corner talking to Freddie Suarez and looked, Sam thought idly, way too serious. But then, the two lawmen were probably talking shop.

A sad smile curved Sam's mouth as he realized that he should be a happy man. He had the family he'd always craved. Hell, he now had enough aunts, uncles, cousins and half-siblings to populate a small city. And more importantly, he'd won custody of his daughters.

So if everything was going so great, why was he so miserable? Stupid question, he thought. He knew damn well why he was miserable. Because he *deserved* to be. He took a long swig of his cold beer and felt it hit his stomach like a hard ball of lead. Grimacing, he set the beer down atop a tray carried by a passing waiter, then shifted his gaze across the crowd again, looking for one woman. One face.

He spotted her from across the room. Michelle was climbing the stairs to the second story. Hand on the banister, she kept her face averted from the crowd below, but, as she took the curve in the sweeping stairwell, Sam saw the pain she'd hidden so well today. *Follow her, you idiot,* his heart seemed to be telling him. And for the first time in too long, he shut off the rational, logical voice in his head and listened to what he should have all along.

The heart that had first led him to Michelle. The heart that still needed her so badly.

"You're an idiot if you let her go," he told himself. For the past ten years, he'd mourned her loss. He'd been haunted by what-could-have-beens. And now, he had the chance to rewrite history. To make all of those old dreams come true. Would he really give that all away for the sake of *pride?*

Decision made, he went after her. As he should have when she first walked away. Grim determination set his jaw as he moved through the crowd slowly, excusing himself and gently nudging the people out of his way. Gaze still locked on the staircase that would take him to Michelle, he watched Inspector Suarez take the stairs two at a time in long, hurried strides.

An unnamed fear settled low in his belly, and instinct prodded Sam to quicken his pace. Forgetting politeness in his rush to get to Michelle, he put his head down and bulled his way through the crush of wedding guests.

At the top of the stairs, Michelle started down the carpeted hall toward Miranda's room. Grateful to be away from all of the people and the rampant happiness for a few minutes, she lifted one hand to rub at her temple in an effort to calm the headache that wouldn't go away. She just wanted to make sure her friend's going-away outfit was laid out so there wouldn't be any delays. Just because her own short-lived marriage was ending so badly was no reason to let anything go wrong for Miranda and Daniel.

A pang of regret ricocheted around the edges of her heart, and she told herself grimly to get used to it. "It's your own fault," she muttered as anger mingled with the pain, "for falling in love with such a hardheaded man. You couldn't pick out someone reasonable, oh no. *You* had to want a pigheaded Marine."

Gritting her teeth, she stopped outside Miranda's closed door and told herself to keep smiling. Soon, the wedding would be over and she could go home. To pack. Oh my, yes, there was a cheery thought.

She stepped inside and came to an abrupt stop.

"Leeza?" she said, her gaze locked on the woman across the room from her.

The big, blowsy blonde slowly swiveled her head to stare at her. "What are you doing up here?" she asked, her features twisted into a disgusted scowl.

"I was about to ask you the same thing," Michelle said just as she noticed Miranda's now-empty jewelry box lying upended on the dressing table. Outrage shimmered inside her as she accused, "You're *stealing* Miranda's jewels?"

"Well now," Leeza murmured, turning to point a completely intimidating pistol at Michelle's middle, "it's a damn shame you had to stumble in here." Then she shrugged wide shoulders, lifting her abundant bosom into a massive heave. "Wrong place, wrong time, darlin'."

Michelle looked from the black hole of the gun barrel up into Leeza's cold eyes and knew she was in big trouble. But strangely enough, her fear wasn't strong enough to keep her quiet. "You've got a *gun?*" She paused and then whispered, "It was you, wasn't it?"

"What do you mean?"

Everything in Sam went cold and still when he heard through the closed door Michelle mention that Leeza had a gun.

Sweet God! Ice covered his insides and he threw a glance at the open doorway. From downstairs, music and muted conversations drifted through the air, making this whole scene feel surreal. This wasn't happening. Michelle really wasn't in that room with an unstable woman holding a gun.

In a flash of images, the future stretched out in front of him. Sam saw himself. Raising the girls alone. Going through the rest of his life without ever hearing Michelle's laughter again. Without touching her, holding her. Emptiness roared through him, and Sam knew he couldn't do it. Couldn't face being without her again. He wouldn't lose her. Not this time.

He nudged Suarez, but the man only shook his head *no* and held one finger to his lips. How in the hell could the man just sit here, listening? Didn't he realize that Michelle was in danger?

Panic reared up and tore at his throat, but Sam held perfectly still. He called up every ounce of Marine training he'd ever had to keep him calm. Logical. Rational. And it wasn't working. He was willing to give Inspector Suarez a minute or two more to hear what he obviously wanted to hear. But the minute that conversation shifted—the minute Michelle's life was at stake—Sam was going through that door if he had to plow right over the law to do it.

"You poisoned Ryan Fortune," Michelle said.

Leeza smiled. "What the hell, I can tell you. It's not like you'll be running downstairs to spread the word, huh?'' She laughed then, and the harsh sound grated like fingernails on a blackboard. "Yeah, that was me. And if the old bastard had died like he was supposed to, I wouldn't be standing here settling for chump change out of this jewelry box."

"Why would you kill him?" Michelle asked, while a part of her hoped that if she kept Leeza talking long enough, *someone* might come upstairs in time to save her life.

The other woman motioned with the gun, waving Michelle farther into the room. "It was Lloyd's idea. Naturally it didn't work. That man never could do anything right."

"I don't understand," Michelle told her, although she did, clearly.

Leeza snorted and, keeping one eye on Michelle, scooped up her handbag and slung it across her shoulder. "Lloyd figured that if Ryan was dead, Miranda would get a bigger cut of the Fortune money. Hell, you've seen how these people live. Why should they miss a few million? I slipped the digitalis into the port decanter during that first big party. Cracked me up, watching the law try to pin it on one of the new Fortune heirs." She shook her head and smiled, as if at a fond memory. Then the smile faded into a mask of disgust. "The plan would have worked fine if that stubborn old coot had just died like he was supposed to."

"But he didn't."

"Nope." Leeza shook her head, and her brittle blond hair swung about her face like hanks of ratty twine. "Then Lloyd kicks off, and I'm left high and dry." Clearly disgusted, she shrugged again and said, "So what's a girl like me gonna do? It ain't like I'm getting any younger, you know. Haven't got many good years left. So, I figure I'll take what I can and split."

"Where'll you go?" Michelle swallowed hard and glanced fast around the room, looking for a place to hide from a bullet. Unfortunately, the bed ruffle didn't look as though it was bulletproof.

"Not as far as I would have," Leeza told her. "But once I pawn these jewels, I should be set for a while. And once you're out of the way, I'll be able to get out of town long before anybody notices these little doodads are gone."

"Miranda will notice right away," Michelle told her, not really knowing if that would help her case or hurt it. Still, while Leeza was talking, she wasn't shooting, so that was a good thing. *Sam, damn it, why aren't you looking for me? I need you.*

"She's so wrapped up in that new hubby of hers, she couldn't care less about a few stones." Leeza lifted the gun a bit higher and Michelle looked straight down that black barrel. "The question is, what do I do about you?"

"I think I can answer that question," Inspector

Suarez said flatly as he stepped into the room, gun drawn and pointed at Leeza.

Sam was right behind the lawman, and Michelle's knees almost buckled with the relief swamping her.

"Well, damn it all to hell," Leeza muttered.

"That about sums it up," Suarez said and added, "Drop the gun, Leeza. You're not going anywhere."

She seemed to think about it for a long moment, then resignedly tossed her pistol onto the bed. "I never should have listened to Lloyd," she said, to no one in particular. "Ever since I came to Texas, I've had nothing but bad luck."

Sam's heart started beating again the moment he dropped one arm around Michelle's shoulders and pulled her close. When she leaned into him, it was all he could do to keep from holding her tight enough to crack a rib. But then, a man didn't often have to survive his wife being held hostage by a crazy woman.

"I think the Fortunes would argue about just whose luck turned bad when you showed up in town," Freddie said. "Toss your purse onto the bed and put your hands behind your back."

"Miranda's jewelry is in her purse," Michelle told him.

"Yeah I know," he said, shooting her a quick grin. "I was listening at the door. Heard everything."

"Well, that tears it," Leeza said, and stood still

while Suarez slapped a pair of handcuffs on her wrists.

As he led his prisoner toward the door, the Inspector glanced back at Sam and Michelle. "I'll need you two to make a statement."

"Tomorrow?" Sam asked.

"Fine." Then he said, "Come on now, Leeza. I think you'll like the San Antonio jail."

She grumbled a bit, but no one was paying any attention. When they were gone, and Michelle and Sam were alone again, silence dropped on the room like a heavy blanket. She inhaled the scent of him and took it deep inside her, hoping to capture the memory of it so that something of him would always be with her. Only moments ago, she'd been standing too close to death and now, with Sam holding her, she felt more alive than she had in years.

He turned her into his chest, wrapped both arms around her and held on tight. "I don't think I've ever been that scared in my life."

"Me either. Boy, was I glad to see you." Michelle's arms snaked around his middle, and she let herself enjoy the sensation of being pressed against him. For a few minutes there, she hadn't been at all sure she'd ever see him again, let alone know the simple joy of holding him.

"Michelle," he said, and pulled her back from him far enough that he could look down into her eyes. The pads of his thumbs caressed her cheekbones and she felt the warmth of his touch down into the darkest corners of her soul. She'd missed him so much. Needed him so much.

"Michelle, I love you. I always have."

Her breath hitched, but he wasn't finished.

"I've been stubborn and stupid and damn near lost you through my own bullheadedness." His gaze moved over her features like a caress. "You were right. What you said to me that last time. It's killed me to realize that I wasted the time we might have had together because I was too proud—and too gutless—to chase you down and demand an answer. Then when I finally got the answers I wanted, my pride got in the way again. Damn it, Michelle, we've both made mistakes...but let's not make anymore."

"Sam—"

"No," he interrupted, "let me finish. I have to say this. Have to make you see. Understand. When I knew you were in danger and I couldn't get to you—" He shook his head and gave her a half smile. "I almost clobbered Freddie to get in here. All I could think about was reaching you."

Her breath caught in her chest, and hope blossomed in her heart.

"I don't care about the past anymore," he was saying. "And I don't have any pride left. All I'm interested in is the future. *Our* future."

"Sam—"

"Don't say no," he interrupted her and kept talking, words pouring out of him in a rush. "Not yet, anyway. At least think about it. I want to be your husband, Michelle. I've *always* wanted that. I want us to be together. To raise the girls. To be a family, like we were always meant to be. Give me a chance," he said, and bent to place a quick, tender kiss on her lips. "I can't live without you again. I love you so much. Give me a chance to do it right this time. Don't say no."

Joy bubbled through her veins like fine champagne. Her hardheaded, proud, stubborn Marine was offering her the world, and he looked as though he was afraid she might not want it. Reaching up, she cupped his face in her hands and shook her head. "Foolish man," she whispered, "how could you ever think I'd say no? I *love* you. That's forever."

He sighed, turned his face into her hand and kissed her palm. "Forever," he murmured, then bent to claim a kiss that would seal their love, their marriage and make it everything they had ever wanted.

* * * * *

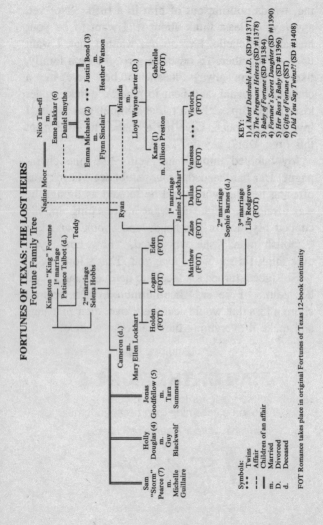

SOME MEN ARE BORN TO BE ROYALTY.
OTHERS ARE MADE...

CROWNED HEARTS

A royal anthology featuring,
NIGHT OF LOVE, a classic novel from
international bestselling author

DIANA PALMER

Plus a brand-new story in the MacAllister family series by

JOAN ELLIOT PICKART

and a brand-new story by

LINDA TURNER

which features the royal family of the upcoming
ROMANCING THE CROWN series!

Available December 2001 at your favorite retail outlet.

Where love comes alive™

PSCH

Coming in January 2002 from Silhouette Books...

THE GREAT MONTANA COWBOY AUCTION

by
ANNE McALLISTER

With a neighbor's ranch at stake, Montana-cowboy-turned-Hollywood-heartthrob Sloan Gallagher agreed to take part in the Great Montana Cowboy Auction organized by Polly McMaster. Then, in order to avoid going home with an overly enthusiastic fan, he provided the money so that Polly could buy him and take him home for a weekend of playing house. But Polly had other ideas....

Also in the Code of the West

Available at your favorite retail outlet.

Silhouette®
Where love comes alive™

Visit Silhouette at www.eHarlequin.com

PSGMCA

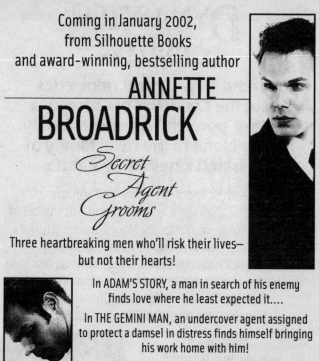

DYNASTIES:
THE
CONNELLYS

A brand-new Desire® miniseries about the Connellys of Chicago, a wealthy, powerful American family tied by blood to the royal family of the island kingdom of Altaria

Filled with scandal, mystery and romance, *Dynasties: The Connellys* will keep you enthralled in 12 wonderful new stories by your favorite authors, including Leanne Banks, Kathie DeNosky, Caroline Cross, Maureen Child, Kate Little, Metsy Hingle, Kathryn Jensen, Kristi Gold, Cindy Gerard, Katherine Garbera, Eileen Wilks and Sheri WhiteFeather.

Don't miss
this exciting program,
beginning in January 2002 with:

TALL, DARK & ROYAL
by Leanne Banks
(SD #1412)

*Available at your
favorite retail outlet.*

Where love comes alive™